BITTER OVER SWEET

Melissa Llanes Brownlee

sfwp.com

Library of Congress Cataloging-in-Publication Data pending

Names: Llanes Brownlee, Melissa, 1974- author
Title: Bitter over sweet / Melissa Llanes Brownlee.
Description: Santa Fe : Santa Fe Writers Project, 2025. | Summary:
  "Hawaiian native Tita works to escape a vicious cycle of poverty and
  abuse, only to realize along the way that life can not only be better,
  it can be whatever she wants it to be... Take a deep dive into the lives
  of real Hawaiians as we follow Tita and other native women living and
  struggling against abuse and despair in a world controlled by tourism's
  long tail. These stories of resilience offer readers a glimpse behind
  the bird-of-paradise curtains and a look at what's not in the travel
  magazines. What is it like to live day in and day out in a place that
  everyone else considers paradise? To live within America but not be
  considered American enough?"—Provided by publisher.
Identifiers: LCCN 2024058708 (print) | LCCN 2024058709 (ebook) |
  ISBN 9781951631512 trade paperback | ISBN 9781951631529 ebook
Subjects: LCGFT: Novels
Classification: LCC PS3612.L35 B58 2025 (print) | LCC PS3612.L35 (ebook) |
  DDC 813/.6—dc23/eng/20250310
LC record available at https://lccn.loc.gov/2024058708
LC ebook record available at https://lccn.loc.gov/2024058709

Published by SFWP
369 Montezuma Ave. #350
Santa Fe, NM 87501
www.sfwp.com

Contents

Trophies

We don't take food stamps for that, the cashier frowns. Her red lipstick seeps into the cracks around the pale edges of her lips as I grip the flimsy brown note my mother gave me to buy her a couple of cigarettes, *menthol if they got 'em.* I put on my best I'm about to cry face, knowing that if I don't get these cigarettes, I'll really have something to cry about. The cashier doesn't soften, her face as hard as her blonde Aqua Net bouffant, and I think about dropping to the floor and sobbing but figure that might be too much. I do the downcast eyes and tiny shoulder shakes that may, if not dealt with quickly, erupt into a full-blown volcano, hoping the clerk doesn't want to deal with a little brown girl in a torn black t-shirt and ripped Dove shorts from the Goodwill, having a meltdown in the middle of the only drugstore on the mountain. The local coffee farmers and coffee workers, pulling in for snacks or necessities that they don't want to drive into town for, wonder why the cashier won't just sell the cigarettes for the single brown food stamp like they know she should, and one of them takes pity on me and pays for the cigarettes and adds a chocolate bar to the mix. The sun shines from my face as I tuck the brown single in my shorts so my mother doesn't see it and I carry my trophies out to the old car my mother got from a friend, her leg propped on the open window, her foot tapping against the sky. *You had better have gotten menthols,* she says as she pulls the paper bag towards her, and I hide the chocolate behind my back.

The Black Box
She's Only Seen on TV

Cousin has a brand-new Atari in the living room. Tita chomps on her creme crackers, smothered in margarine. She dunks them in hot cocoa, oily clumps escaping to the surface with each dip. She pretends she doesn't want to play it. She wants more crackers and butter and cocoa but she wants Pac-Man even more. She gobbles up all the pellets as she drinks—the largest one, giving her power to eat all the blue obake. You can play Atari when you pau breakfast, Tita, Cousin says as she drinks her coffee. Tita smiles and says mahalo Aunty as she finishes her cocoa and crackers, a breakfast she could never have at home, where it was dry wheat toast and hot Lipton tea because everyone was on a diet, including Tita.

Her parents would never buy her an Atari. They don't even buy her Barbies. All their money goes to her older sister, for clothes and cars, for proms and cheerleading. They had sent Tita down south to her Cousin's ranch so they could help her sister prepare for her junior prom with the quarterback of the football team. Even Tita's father was washing and cleaning the car so he could chauffeur them, like he was a taxi driver instead of a cook at a hotel. She didn't understand why her sister got everything she ever wanted but Tita knew they were different. Her sister only ever talked to her when she wanted Tita to do something, iron my dress, clean my room, wash my clothes on delicate. Tita began to wonder if Cinderella was really a true story.

Tita washes her hands in the big kitchen sink, tippy toeing to reach the handles. She had to use a stool at home to wash and dry the dishes but she didn't want to bother Cousin. She soaps off all the margarine as quickly as she can. She doesn't want to get the joystick all greasy. The obake would surely get her if she does. Tita, make sure you get under your nails too. Okay, Aunty. She spends a little more time than she wants under the hot water and then she shakes her hands and rubs them against her favorite blue rainbow t-shirt. She tries not to run to the living room as Cousin follows her to turn on the TV and check that the dial is set to the correct channel. The black box she's only seen on TV and two joysticks sit on the carpet, waiting for her to insert the Pac-Man cartridge into the slot, which she does, settling down, front and center. She flicks the switch on the Atari as Cousin sits on the couch behind her, Pac-Man and the ghosts dancing across the screen as Tita pushes the start button and begins to play.

daddy, he wen put limu in the fish's belly

the fish he wen catch yesterday, so I can win the kids' fishing tournament, I no like catch fish and I no like be in the fishing tournament, but daddy keeps making me go fish, keeps making me go with my bamboo pole out on the lava rocks, the surf spraying us, trying for sweep us out to sea, and I like let 'em, because daddy keeps trying for teach me how to hold the bamboo pole, daddy keeps trying for teach me how to fish and daddy, he wen put limu in the fish's belly because I no can catch fish, no can hold the bamboo pole and I no like go catch fish, but daddy, he make me go, mommy, she no care I one girl, she stay get my other sisters for worry about, Tita, you go with your daddy and catch plenty fish for tomorrow's dinner, and daddy, he takes me fishing at night in the dark, only kerosene light and flashlights, and daddy, he help me hold the bamboo pole and daddy, he wen put limu in the fish's belly, because I no like catch fish and I no like go with daddy

Grover

Your tiny fingers gouge out the eyes of the furry blue creature they placed in your lap to make you smile while your sisters sit around you, their own smiles plastered on their faces, eyes searching for approval. You offer your prize, the discarded and eyeless carcass splayed across your prettiest dress, to the cameraman, the halo of light glinting off your teeth that haven't come loose yet, waiting for strings and doorknobs to yank them out.

The One Who Lies in Wait

My son was born a shark. Mother told me we had to return him to the ocean as soon as he swam out of my birthing sea, his thrashing fins marking their passage along my canal, an explosion of salt and blood, soaking the woven mats beneath me. His father was a sprinkling of sea foam across the mounds of my thighs. I was not as fecund as Mother but I knew when the waves crashed on me that I was pregnant. I hadn't wanted a baby. I wasn't ready. Mother told me it was the way of our kind. As she birthed me from an infusion of light from Father, stars spiraling from her belly, so will I birth the gods of land and sea. As I cradled my first child, his cool gray skin rubbing against me, his dark intelligent eyes settling on mine, I knew the burden and the triumph of birthing a god. I kissed the tip of his nose as I walked to the edge of the water and released him into the salty embrace of his father.

Avon Calling You an Autumn When You Know You Are Summer

Ah you're an autumn she says as I eye the shadows and mouth the names on the lipstick tubes, buttered rum, precious pearl, amorous rose, cool peach, every word a pucker.

What's autumn? We had to clean the house spic and span before she came over because mom didn't want her thinking we were dirty and poor.

She is carefully unloading her samples on the glass coffee table in the special living room for company, her soft white hands, tipped in a tasteful nude, she would later tell my mom. Oh, you know, it's fall, when the leaves fall.

Leaves fall? My mother shakes her head. Her teased and permed hair hardened by hairspray. Her eyes rimmed black. Her brows brushed and darkened. Her lips an appropriate red for her job at the bank.

Yes, off of trees when they turn red, orange or yellow.

Leaves don't change colors here. She stops and looks at me, seeing my dark brown skin and long tangled brown hair, my favorite rainbow t-shirt and not matching shorts, my long legs, scratched and scarred from playing in the sun all year long.

I guess you are right, but still, you are an autumn, dear. She clicks her emptied case closed.

Far, Far Away

The launch is beautiful, white plumes spreading. We hold our breath, all of us little kids with makapiapia and stars in our eyes, hopes of Space Camp buzzing through our brains. We imagine zero G simulators and talking robots who help us fly to space. We woke up early before school, bowls of Frosted Flakes, Lucky Charms, Fruit Loops, Apple Jacks, Fruity Pebbles in our laps as we sat in front of our TVs, parents sitting on couches, sipping coffee. We learned there was a teacher onboard but we were cheering for the boy from Kona, the boy who became an astronaut. The boy we all wanted to be, even our parents. His own parents so proud, working in their general store on the mountain, handing out crack seed and kettle chips to us kids when we drove by in the back of our fathers' trucks. As we watch him fly higher, our dreams follow him, one day we would be working on space stations, mining the moon, flying to the asteroids and Saturn and Jupiter and maybe even, one day, another galaxy, far, far away. We dip our spoons into our bowls as the sky parts.

may day is lei day in Hawai'i

plumeria strangle Tita's neck, pink, white, yellow petals, plucked the night before from the neighbor's tree, its branches dangling across their fence and over the sidewalk, their smell invading her sunstroked nostrils, piercing her may day haze of queen and princesses and bazaar foods of pickle mango, malasadas, stone cookies, hot dogs, and she shakes her unbrushed hair, hearing her mother how you going leave the house, looking down at her favorite rainbow t-shirt, the edges frayed, and hefts her school ukulele, readying for her grade's performance of a medley of the islands, the koa edges soft and hard against her bare thighs, her okole still sore from the last you better, her knees scabbed from flying from the tallest swing on the playground, my dog has fleas singing in her ears

Menehune

They built the walls and the fishponds, my tutu tells me one day when I ask who they were after seeing the uncles fish beers from the coolers. They could build an entire structure in one night, the villagers and chiefs, waking up to a fishpond ready to be stocked with fish, a wall separating ahupua'a, my tutu tells me as he picks up poke with chopsticks, bits of inamona and limu clinging to the freshly caught ahi.

That didn't explain why the one on the beer bottle kept talking to me, his pudgy face, his short little malo, his bare chest, a flower over his ear, his hand in a permanent shaka. I get beer in my ear, he would say over and over, his smile spreading wider and wider, between the darkened and gnarled fingers of the uncles.

Are they leprechauns? I ask, thinking about pots of gold at the end of rainbows and Lucky Charms, marshmallows floating in a milky rainbow. Do you think leprechauns live in Hawai'i? He asks, laughing and almost choking on his poke. No Keone, they are not leprechauns. They don't wear green. They don't wear hats. They don't live at the end of rainbows, and they don't have gold.

Then, who are they? Now, that's a good question. He picks up the bottle of beer, the one that keeps talking to me, I can see its eyes peeking at me between my tutu's fingers. He shows me the bottle. This is what everyone thinks they are. Like leprechauns, tiny, cute, useful. Everyone loves a cute mascot. He wraps his hand around the bottle, hiding the smirking menehune from me.

I think they are the people who were living here first. Living here first? We were first. That's what they teach us at school. Oh really? You think we were the only ones who could sail here? No? I think others came first, and when we came, we were stronger and bigger and had more than them, but they had already built fishponds and walls, so we just kept them and used their skills to make more.

I get beer in my ear, I hear it say, muffled in my Tutu's hands. I get beer in my ear, and I wonder what will happen to us when someone bigger and stronger and has more will do to us.

Cookies

My mother has a thing about jars, not canning jars filled with fresh fruit and vegetable harvests, but gallon jars filled with her obsessions: a rainbow of paper cranes, folded for health, their creases, knifed edges, pressed against glass, pink fake sugar packets first dumped into her purse, then their saggy bodies shoved to fit all the way to the top, thumbtacks ripped from signboards, silver and gold sparkling sharp in their new cage. They line the shelves in our kitchen. Every Sunday, we pull each one down, soapy water in the sink, washing away the dust of the week. Desiccated bodies of spiders, legs curled around each other, collected with tweezers from the corners of our house, greet us. Crushed saltines in plastic, compressed with each new addition, my mother insisting she can fit one more in. We wash. We rinse. We dry. I try not to stare into each jar, each obsession stranger than the last, wishing my mother filled them with normal things like pasta, or oatmeal or even cookies. I dream of jars filled with chocolate chips freshly baked, Oreos freshly bought. As she puts each jar back in its place, positioning it just right, her eyes manic bright, her fingers tracing lines and legs and edges, I stare out the kitchen window, wishing the glass would break.

go get da fish bat

my mother screams at me, the same scream she uses when she's about to give me dirty lickins but I know I didn't do anything wrong, so I run to the carport and get the fish bat out of the back seat of my older sister's car she says she uses for protection from crazy hitchhikers, but I don't know why she even picks up hitchhikers, hasn't she seen any movies about hitchhikers who stalk you and kill you, but my sister says, *you stay lolo, no get killah hitchhikers,* but you never know, they fly in crazy homeless people all the time from the mainland, and I run back into the house with the fish bat and my mom's eyes never leave the floor and I see why she screamed at me, she's staring down the longest centipede I have ever seen, almost one foot, and I want to scream too, but I know my mother would use the fish bat on me instead, and the centipede hasn't noticed us yet, it's still slithering along the wall in our living room, and I pass the fish bat to my mother, trying to get as far away from the creeping, crawly thing as I can, when all of a sudden, it heads straight for me and I scream and try to run outside again, and its tiny legs ripple across the carpet, and I think about static electricity and if centipedes feel it, and my mother takes the fish bat, which is twice as long as the centipede and whacks it, hard, but it keeps trying to head towards me, its tail whipping to sting the bat, and I hold in my next scream, because crying after getting lickins is much worse, and my mother whacks the head and the tail whips up to sting the bat again, but now it's stuck to the carpet and my mother keeps hitting it over and over and over, and I know I will have to clean what's left

Regret

It's dark and cool. Lights are flashing in the ceiling. There's a gravestone in front of you. You read Michael Myers and feel thunder shake your young body. You aren't scared. You look down and there is no ground under the rickety walkway, just black goop, and you think it's probably blood.

You regret asking the waiter for real rice at the Chinese restaurant your auntie took you to when they placed white rice on the lazy susan and it wasn't sticky but fluffy, an array of gravy covered egg foo yong, thin slices of charsiu, beef broccoli, surrounding it. You beg for ketchup and shoyu, and your auntie laughs as you bow your head in shame.

You regret getting lost with your sister in Knott's Berry Farm when your auntie specifically told you to meet everyone at the fried chicken restaurant out front by six, but you were having too much fun, riding the Corkscrew and pretending you were weightless on the Parachute Sky Jump, your slippers scrunched between your toes so they wouldn't fly off as you dangled in the sky. She pulls your ear hard when you finally meet them. You try not to cry and you want to bow your head, shamed.

You regret digging a bobby pin in your ears when flying from Hawai'i because it didn't help them pop, not knowing that all you needed was a stick of Double Mint or Big Red and you'd be feeling better in no time. Your auntie tries to smack some sense into you, your head as sore as your ears, and you hide your head in shame as the stewardess looks away.

You regret not riding Space Mountain more than two times, the darkness, welcoming and inviting, the lights, stars and galaxies you dream of visiting, the music sending chills through your little body. Your blood sings as you exit the ride each time. The second time your auntie screams at you to move your ass or you will miss the parade, and you shake your head, looking around, ashamed of her.

You regret not knowing how to pray when you are with the auntie and uncle and the cousins in the hotel room at night before bed, the words flowing so easily from their tongues. You sheepishly say God is Love and bow your head to hide your shame.

You close your eyes and worry that it will make it worse, your auntie behind you as you walk through the Halloween exhibit at the Hollywood Wax Museum. You take a deep breath, knowing that even wax could come alive and get you, exiting into the Nightmare on Elm Street, Freddy's finger knives hovering, and you tell yourself, you regret nothing.

A Ghost under the Kitchen Sink

Tita's mom has Tita's bed facing away from the door because that's how the devil enters your body when you are asleep and the devil would like nothing better than to possess a girl like you from your toes right on up to your head. So, her bed is against the wall under the window she isn't allowed to open because evil spirits like to come in, especially when your room isn't clean. Sometimes, she likes to look into the darkness and catch a glimpse of any spirit trying to enter her room, imagining a swirl of hair and glinty eyes.

Tita must always keep her room immaculately clean, especially under her bed, because ghosts feel welcome if they have clothes and towels and books and bags to hide among. Ghosts want to grab you and pull you under there, taking you to their world. She imagines a dark-haired girl with unblinking eyes grinning at her, waiting to pull her down as she looks under her bed to check if it's clean, knowing that the things under her bed have nothing to do with ghosts.

Tita never puts her purse on the floor even in her room. Always hang your purse on a chair or on a hook. Spirits will steal your luck and take all of your money. She doesn't really have any money but she knows that when she does, she will lose it as quickly as she gets it even if her purse never touches the ground.

Tita's parents tell her not to whistle at night. They will get you if you whistle. Evil spirits love to take little girls who whistle at night. They tell her not to clip her fingernails at night too. Dark witches love to collect your bits and use them to curse you. So, she is always careful to never whistle no matter how much she wants to and to bury her fingernail clippings in the bottom of the trash where no witch can find them.

When Tita's parents leave her at home one night, she absolutely knows there is a ghost under the kitchen sink full of dishes she was supposed to wash and dry and put away and she runs across the street to the neighbors, crying and shaking, snot streaming down her nose and into her mouth, hiccupping about dark hair and dark eyes behind the bottle of dish soap. When her parents come home to a house with the doors open, all of the lights on, the dishes still dirty in the sink and no Tita, the neighbors try to bring her back but she is screaming about the girl under the kitchen sink and crumples on the neighbors' perfectly green lawn, knowing that there are worse things than a ghost under the kitchen sink.

Bitter over Sweet

God damn it! Stay get worms in the damn powdered milk from da government surplus again! Aunty screamed into the white box with black writing. *Kids, you going have to pull them all out or you not going get milk with your cereal for breakfast.* She lays a clean sheet on the table, and we all sit down as she shakes the box out, snowy drifts and cloudy puffs almost coating our dark skin. *Make sure you get em all. You no like eat em.* We carefully pluck out white little bodies, a bowl on the table to catch our prizes. *No forget for count em. You going get one spoon of honey if you get da most.* Our eager fingernails fill with dust as we dream of sweetness on our tongues. Then we remember the last time we got honey from the government, and the crystals leave a bitter taste in our mouths.

The First Word

The wrong dress, floral and pink, worn to a failed interview for a school she will never be able to enter, dumped in the Goodwill box. The torn song sheet from a missed audition, because her mother forgot to pick her up, burned and buried behind the house. The portable cd player, she'd bought with her own birthday money, stolen by her sister to use in her new car their parents bought because she was dating a quarterback and needed a car for cheerleading practice and a part time job. The broken-lock diary her brother ripped from her hands to tease her about her first crush, his cruel words burned red as the hearts she'd drawn, tossed in the trash after his fun. The fantasy books, she borrowed from the library, used to hold up the couch her dad insisted he would fix before they were due. The old typewriter, a gift from the aunt who lives too far away to know, resold to an antique shop before she could even type.

The Devil You Don't Know

The devil will enter your body if you sleep with your feet to the door. He likes to hop in bodies. He knows how easy it is, especially with girls like you, my mother warns as she pulls my ponytail tight, brush bristles scraping my scalp, revenge for all of the ukus she had to comb out and wash too many times with the uku shampoo.

The devil enters bodies. He likes children who don't listen. Children who don't cook the rice when they get home. Children who watch TV and don't clean the bathroom or wash their laundry before their mothers get home, she yells, clutching the wooden spoon in her hand.

The devil likes bodies, especially bodies like yours that should be hidden, covered.

The devil wants to enter your body, she whispers as she moves your bed so your feet face the door, *because he knows what kind of girl you are.* You can't move. She's strapped you in tight, so the bed bugs don't bite, the edges of the sheet holding you down.

The devil enters your body as she watches, the triumph ablaze in her eyes. He enters through your toes. You can feel a warmth spread upwards, a fiery hug of nerve endings and muscle fibers. He moves slow, in time to your heart, slowing your breath, calming you. You watch her triumph die as the devil smiles with your lips and you join him with your eyes.

Holoholo

My long legs clamber over the hot edge of dad's yellowed Datsun truck, its high-rise tires making it better than any jungle gym on my school's playground. I claim the tire hump on the left before my little sister can scam her way there with a lift from our dad. On the left, you can pretend to be driving down the highway, wind whipping your hair away from your face, a cigarette dangling from your fingertips, the ash waiting to burn those behind you.

Dad wants to go holoholo. The empty white food buckets he took from work still smell like gutted manini and menpachi from the last time he went fishing. They're stacked up against the rear window, his throw net shoved inside the top, the weights along its edge the only thing keeping it in there. His poles are strapped tight over the right tire hump so my sister has to sit next to the stinky buckets and she gives me even stinkier eyes, but I don't care. I'm ready to go.

We race out of our pastel neighborhood of cookie cutter houses towards the highway, passing the school and the other not so pastel neighborhoods. The road turns from scrubby bushes and vine draped trees into rolling lava fields as we head towards the ever-present gleam of the ocean.

I don't even feel the heat of the morning sun behind my back as I face into the wind, my hair streaming behind me. I keep my eyes wide for as long as I can, daring the wind to burn them clean and new.

The tires pull against the highway as we slow down to turn onto the unpaved road to the shore. The salt blows softly against my face as we stop and dad gets out to turn on the truck's four-wheel drive. I'm glad he didn't ask me to do it because I am pretty sure my sister would have stolen my seat.

Dad gets back in and off we go, the rocks and sand grinding and bumping below us. Dad swings left and right, finding the best path among the bad ones. I think about letting go of the sides of the truck like I've seen on the roller coasters on TV, but I remember the one time someone's dog went flying out of the back of their truck and rolled under their wheel. Its little white body merging with the white sand. We were all shocked to see it was fine but it still scared us.

The ride is over when dad pulls into his favorite spot, a little white beach next to shimmering tide pools, perfect for throwing net. I stand and stretch my legs, staring out at the highways of blue and gray flowing to the horizon.

Wheel of Fortune

Tutu took a bottle of fish sauce and the only green mango left and draped the curtain between us in the kitchenette and his cubby hole. My mother rolled her eyes at him and then me, turning up the little black and white TV so we couldn't hear him slicing and dicing and dipping. I was mad he had taken the last green mango. Uncle had brought over a bag from his neighbor's tree and mom had pickled some, leaving one lonely mango next to the bananas and papayas. I wanted to savor the salty sour fishy flavors myself. I would have shared. But tutu, he never shared. We watched Pat Sajak and Vanna White, my mother guessing the words and phrases before the letters were turned, yelling at the stupid contestants. Out of the corner of my eye, I could see the curtain moving in and out with a rhythm that wasn't mango eating and I quickly looked at the TV again to stare at Vanna's pearly smile and sparkly gown, closing my ears to anything but applause and Pat's comments.

When the eye of Hurricane ʻIwa is passing over us

we all drive through feet of ocean on Aliʻi Drive, our wheels fanning the water as we watch houses release their contents into the raging surf: chairs, couches, tables, and we laugh, our faces pressed against the cars' windows, witnessing other people's dreams wash away, our own, safe, on the mountain, far from our ocean, and we wonder if anyone is even there to save their precious things, but we all know they will just buy more, and we stop laughing, returning home before the eye stops watching us.

tangerine

She pulls a tangerine from the tree in the center of the yard, not-garden. Spiraled shells embedded in broken, spindly coral, hard packed into nearly flat stones, formed in the constant continental drift of the Pacific, half-buried in the red volcanic dirt, circle the tree, a path made by mom and dad in a fury. "No! Dig here! Here! And here!" Citrus sprays her face and fingers, orange pith and peels fall, as the earth shivers on her tongue.

to da lady who stay looking down her high makamaka nose at us

what you stay looking at anyway Are we not dressed appropriately for the grocery store? *what?* Should we not have bare feet, crusted with sand, or dirt, or mud? *you never see kids using food stamps?* Are we not rich enough for you with our brown hands gripping colorful paper that is not quite money, given to us by mothers, fathers, aunties, uncles, to get us out of their way? *we not stay making any kind, no need for act like that* Should we bow our heads and be thankful for your presence, for the money you give our mothers and aunties and sisters, for serving your food, cleaning your room, selling you trinkets made in China? *no need for call over the security guard* Are we not grateful enough that you allow us to serve you every day, each paycheck gone as quickly as they are earned, our families working way too long and too hard to afford just to live on our islands? *we stay going*

Tita Likes to Lick Ice Cream in the Dark

She especially likes mint chocolate chip. She imagines the green, a fluorescent wand weaving, leaving traces in the air like sparklers on New Year's Eve, kids screaming and throwing jumping jacks under cars as drivers, with maybe a few too many beers, cruise through neighborhoods on the way to family gatherings overflowing with tables of sushi, sashimi, ham, turkey, grilled steak, teriyaki chicken, kalua pig, chicken long rice, lomilomi salmon, poi, rice, pink and green squares of mochi, but never any ice cream. She hides under her school clothes, hanging in the closet, her mu'umu'u draping her shoulders, the mint coating her tongue, better than Aquafresh toothpaste, the chocolate chips, mountains and ridges to uncover, her lips, her teeth, explorers. She wishes ice cream could last forever, hidden in the back of her closet, always ready and waiting just for her.

White wine spritzer

I say to the bartender my eyes barely peeking over the rim of the plastic cup labeled tips and he starts making your next drink, but all I can think about is the giant gingerbread house I get to destroy soon, my body claiming a shard of wall, a bit of roof, broken candy canes and smooshed gum drops, white icing streaking my red party dress as I crow in triumph over the other kids, claiming my bounty at dad's work party, but all I will remember is our car pulling over, hazards flashing in the dark like broken Christmas lights, your stomach emptying, streaking your matching party dress as you cry, your tears mixing with what's left of the white wine spritzers on the road.

At Night They Open Their Glass Cages

They like to come out at night, Tita said. When everyone was asleep, they would move so slowly, lifting the glass prisons they lived in when on display for Girl's Day or stored in a closet, buried beneath Christmas decorations. Their long fingers pushing and pulling themselves out of their boxes. Then, they would grow their nails long and sharp so that they could cut up and eat the cats and dogs wandering the neighborhood at night, and on very special nights, they would cut up and eat a child. You're lying, I said. I'm not. You remember Jennifer? She used to live three houses down? Her family moved out last month but she never came to say bye. It's because they couldn't find her. All they found was blood on her bed one morning and they got so scared they ran away. Whatever, I said, and Tita pinched me, hard.

Tita liked to tell me scary stories when she was mad, mad at mom, mad at school, mad at her friends. It didn't matter. When she got mad, she made sure I was the one to hear her. She'd stomp into our room and sit on my bed. If I was in the living room or the kitchen, she'd pull me with her. Even in the bathroom, I was not safe. She knew I hated scary stories, especially hers. She'd sit me down on the floor in front of her. No pillow to hug, no teddy bear. I had no dolls because her favorite stories were about the dolls at our neighbor's house.

At night, she'd always start, they would open their glass cages and grow their nails so long and sharp they could cut through the walls, they could cut through glass, but what they really loved to cut through were little girls like you. I would close my eyes when she started her doll stories, and she would always kick me to keep my eyes open and on her. They'd crawl on their razor blade fingers, looking for something to kill, something to eat. Sliding under the doors, their bodies as thin and flexible as their nails. Swish snick swish snick, they crawled along sidewalks, mown lawns, peering through windows, under doors, always hungry, always searching. They'd crawl into bedrooms filled with sleeping children wanting just the right snack. Swish snick swish snick. They'd crawl on top of the bed and snick snick they'd start their slicing and dicing, their little mouths opening wider than their heads, all that was left were bloodstains on the sheets.

Sometimes Tita would wake me up in the middle of the night to tell me they were coming to get me. Get into my bed, she'd tell me. They won't come for you if you're with me. I would get up and follow her too sleepy to protest. The two of us hiding under her covers, together, as I snuggled the doll I never had.

Cruising in Kona

Tita yells at her sister to get out of the water. All the tourists have left and she won't be able to dive for any more coins. Her sister grumbles as she scrambles up the side of the pier. They walk to the showers to wash the salt off, Tita's sister bragging about all of the money she scored from the stupid tourists. Tita rolls her eyes.

They change out of their swimsuits in the bathroom, avoiding the people camped around it. They would have used the hotel's bathroom but you need a room key nowadays. As they leave, they smell a sweet burning scent from a dude in a tank top and shorts, the smell inviting them to join him. They see him sitting under the shade of the banyan tree, his dark lashed eyes closed, a wistful smile on his lips. Tita tells her sister to keep walking.

A man jumps out from behind the tree, yelling at them for being in his house, his broken sunglasses, winking at them as they walk quickly past his patch of ground. Tita protects her sister, blocking the man's approach, ready to swing her bag at him if he gets too close, his rancid breath covering their escape.

A strong breeze clears the air around them and they breathe in relief. They continue along, the seawall, rising above them on the right. A truck speeds past, and they jump against the wall, the wind of its passing, pushing them back the way they had come. A couple snorts at their fear, their matching pink running suits, puffed around them as they jog past.

Tita swears they had died and come back with how close that truck had come to hitting them. She wants to scream at the pink people and their piggy faces, snorting. Tita wants to cross the street when she hears reggae inviting them to shop in air conditioning, but she knows that it's just a tourist trap, charging too much for cheap knockoffs, and they keep going.

When they come to the end of the seawall, Tita's sister tries to pull her to the shaved ice shop, but Tita knows that she will have to pay for it but she only has enough for lunch and not both. Tita sees that the bakery is open too and wants hot fresh malasadas, but that's not lunch, and their mom will be so mad if they had shaved ice or malasadas for lunch, so she pulls her sister along avoiding both places, knowing that the 7-11 will have cheaper and more filling food. Maybe they could even head towards McDonald's for hamburger Happy Meals.

Tita's sister doesn't fight her even though Tita knows she wants to. They finally make it to 7-11 and buy Spam musubis and manapua with enough left over for a Coke and cherry Slurpee and they wait for their mother to get off of work and watch the tourists pass them by, happy to be heading home soon.

Tita's Kuleana

Tita walks me to and from school every day. She doesn't want to but she does it because I am her kuleana. I try not to walk too close. I don't want to make her mad. Even when I am scared of the big black dog at the end of the street that loves to bark and chase us, I walk as far from her as I can because I know she's ashamed to be seen with me, my tangled hair, my dirty jeans, my torn t-shirt, my dirty feet in rubber slippers. I hate that dog. I wish someone would feed it paint water. No, I don't. Someone did that to our chihuahua and she died vomiting up her insides.

The black dog starts barking and jumping up and down when it sees Tita. She walks quickly past its house but it's a dark streak of howling, shooting down the driveway behind her. Then it spots me and turns. I'm too far away from Tita and she just keeps walking, leaving me behind. I want to run but I can't move. All I hear is teeth. All I see is growl. I pee my pants, a gush of liquid pouring down my legs. A rock slams into the side of the black dog that's about to eat me and a tiny yelp escapes from the both of us. Another rock goes sailing over my head but the big black dog is slinking back to its driveway, whining. Tita walks back to me, angry and triumphant. I am crying and snot is running down my nose into my mouth. Tita just holds me until I stop crying and we go home side by side.

This is Not Your Kind of Ghost Story

We were sleeping in the rainforest again. Tita wanted to be outside under the stars, so we packed up the beach mats, blankets and pillows and walked out the screen door, hearing it slap against the house as we headed into the jungle on the edge of our backyard. Tita was never scared. She always knew exactly where to go.

We climbed over the rock wall the uncles had built when Tita was born. Like the walls built by Menehune, nothing held the broken lava pieces together. Tita didn't want to hear anyone's cars out there, so she found a small cleared area far from our house or the road. She said it was best if we didn't hear anyone alive.

Tita lived for these nights. Out here she was free, her long dark hair unbraided, un-ponytailed. My own scalp itchy from too tight rubber bands. I envied Tita's freedom. We laid down our beach mats and then our blankets. The stars stared down at us. Tita stopped speaking and just laid back, waiting. I wanted to close my eyes but I knew that if I did, I would miss it. I pulled my blanket over my head, a hood to protect me.

At first, all I heard were the owls hunting the scurrying things in the bushes. Then, I heard Tita sigh, and then, I saw it. Like I knew I would. Her hair began to swim slowly in the air, strands weaving and dancing. I never asked how or why. These were things that only Tita knew and I felt that she couldn't tell me even if she wanted to.

Lose 10 Pounds in 3 Days

Day 1

Breakfast: black tea or coffee, 1/2 a grapefruit, 1 piece of toast with 1 tablespoon of peanut butter, you are only twelve but your mother insists, and you have to follow the rules exactly or you won't lose any weight, your pants and skirts no longer fitting your once straight but now widening hips, but at least there is peanut butter, you think, as you wish for some guava jam to go with it, your mother sitting next to you sipping her black coffee, grapefruit pith clinging to her painted fingernails

Lunch: black tea or coffee, 1/2 a cup of tuna, 1 piece of dry toast, you can't even have mayo, and you remember the time your mother stretched a whole can of tuna across an entire loaf of bread for lunch for the family with almost half a jar of Best Foods, and your drool moistens that sad piece of toast right up as your mother nibbles on hers

Dinner: black tea or coffee, 3 ounces of lean meat, 1 cup of green beans, 1 cup of carrots, 1 small apple, 1 cup of vanilla ice cream, your mother steams some chicken for you, opens cans of green beans and carrots, the only fresh food is the tiny red apple you wouldn't even give a teacher, at least you get some ice cream even though you wish there was some chocolate Magic Shell on top, your mother making sure you eat everything on your plate before finishing her own

Day 2

Breakfast: black tea or coffee, 1 hard-boiled egg, 1 piece of dry toast, 1/2 a banana, you don't want to wake up, you want hot cocoa and not Lipton, again, you want eggs and bacon and pancakes, your stomach feels so empty as you try to pick up non-existent toast crumbs from your empty plate, stop that your mother scolds as she chokes down her egg

Lunch: black tea or coffee, 1 cup of cottage cheese and six saltine crackers, you hate cottage cheese, but your mother watches you eat every spoonful, the dry and salty crackers standing at attention waiting patiently for their turn next to the photocopy of the Military Diet your mother got from her friend at work

Dinner: black tea or coffee, 2 hot dogs, 1 cup of broccoli, 1/2 a cup of carrots, 1/2 a banana, 1/2 a cup of vanilla ice cream, you are excited for hot dogs but there is no ketchup or mustard or relish, your mother says your lucky to even get two, that's too much food for you, but you must follow the diet exactly or you both won't lose the ten pounds and you look at your body and wonder where the ten pounds will come from as you pinch only skin

Day 3

Breakfast: black tea or coffee, 1 small apple, 1 ounce of cheddar cheese, five saltine crackers, you love cheddar cheese and slice your apple and cheese thinly, place them on each one of your five saltine crackers, pretend it's a sandwich at a fancy tea party in a cute little dress your mother would never buy for you, not at home in your t-shirt and shorts, sitting at your plain brown dining table, your mother doing the same

Lunch: black tea or coffee, 1 hard-boiled egg, 1 piece of dry toast, you wish you had saved some cheese for lunch, you dunk your dry piece of toast into your Lipton until it falls apart, drinking your black tea and bread soup, your mother's eyes never leaving your hands, her own wrapped tightly around her coffee

Dinner: black tea or coffee, 1 cup of tuna, 1 cup of carrots, 1 cup of cauliflower, 1 cup of melon, 1/2 a cup of vanilla ice cream, you are so happy it's the last day that you don't even mind the cauliflower, you mix the melon and ice cream, imagining it is a sundae, your mother pushing her tuna around on her plate

Day 4

You get on the scale in your mother's bathroom and have gained five pounds. Your mother is angry and yells, you cheated, you ate something else, didn't you, and you swear you never did and your mother gets on the scale and you are too scared to look and the next day she puts you both on Slim Fast and you know this will never end...

Planted in Blue

I get to school early because I want to hop on the tall swing set before anyone else, the shiny blue seat waiting to carry me away. There's always a line. No one wants to use the baby swings. The only time anyone uses them is when you throw the swing over the top a few times to make the seat so high that when you swing you can jump really far off of it. I throw my brown paper-bag-covered textbooks on the dirt and slide myself on to the seat. I walk backwards as far as the chain will let me, the seat rising almost past my butt and I jump on. As I go forward and make my legs straight, my slippers fly from my feet and I realize I've been wearing my brother's ugly floppy blue and brown spotted ones. My stomach drops. I tuck my feet and swing back. I don't straighten my legs and I slowly stop moving. No one is there to see me, yet. I stand, my bare feet slapping the dirt. I step up onto the seat and push my body, back and forth. My hands become the chains. My toes are spread wide, planted in blue. My legs go forward. My head goes back. My head goes forward. My legs go back. I keep doing this until I am swimming through the air. I think of nothing else but the brown of the dirt and the blue of the sky.

Black Coral

The heat dances through the coral fronds of Tita's black hair as we walk along the lava fields. Soon we will hit the gravely white sands dotted with naked pink tourists, shrimps stretched and oiled. I don't want to look at them but I dart my eyes along their edges, nipping at differences. Tita tells me to stop staring and keep walking.

When we reach the Queen's Bath, salty and fresh, we tear off our clothes and jump into the cold water, its edges dotted pink. Tita's hair unfurls around her, the tiny shrimp finding purchase along her branches. I want to be one of them.

As she swirls around, I drift, tasting the ocean we can hear over the lip of the bath. Tita will leave for the mainland soon. Like now, the shrimp will cling to her but she won't mind. She will be immovable, anchored here.

Of Being

Your auntie has too many damn kids mom tells me one day over a glass of Chablis. She'd just taken a capsule of Fastin for dinner as she laughs at her cousin living on government cheese and food stamps, cornflakes served with spoonfuls of sugar and powdered milk. Even at an early age, I knew the shame of being poor, of being fat, of being anything my mom thought wasn't classy. On her second glass, she whispers the story of how auntie's mom smothered her last child when she fell asleep, rolling her immense body onto the baby as it nursed. *That's why she has so many kids* mom continues to whisper into her third glass, her slender hands cupping it like the face of a sleeping child.

Skin and Bone

Her toes curling in the sand, Tita counts the shells spiraling beside her. Their bleached bodies, remnants of once-living creatures, wondering if her bones will shine as brightly when she is dead.

"Eh, Tita. You like go swimming." She shakes her head at the boy hovering nearby, his brown skin shimmering. She dreams of slipping it on, her body transformed. She thinks of the freedom such a form would give her, no pinching uncles, drunk on beer, hugging her too tight, no stupid boys pulling her bra strap for fun, laughing at her pain, no worrying about strange men, cruising slowly past, windows rolling down, as she walks home from school, wishing she could hide from all of their leering eyes and wandering hands.

"Fine den. Be like dat." The boy runs off, his body cutting through the surf as he dives beneath the waves and Tita wishes he would stay there, his body forever tumbling.

Mother's Obake Shivers
under Your Bed

It's waiting to reach its impossibly long arms for the shirt you ripped at recess, the one you weren't supposed to wear to school. It wants to trace its knife sharp fingers through notebooks filled with the hundreds of I won't draw in my notebooks during class lines you had to write because you were caught drawing in your math, English, social studies, science notebooks again and again. It's ready to drool over the jeans you bled through, nestling its heart shaped head, veined and bumpy like the red anthuriums in your mother's garden, in the rusty bloom. It craves the tears you'll shed when your mother finds these things under your bed. Its spindly arms and legs ready to grab you and hold you safe among your hidden things.

Tita's Sister's Boyfriend

Tita floats in the pool of her sister's latest boyfriend's house, the sharp smell of chlorine, a halo around her head, the water, a warm blue cocoon, echoing the sky above her. Tita's sister's boyfriend is a chiropractor or something, but she doesn't care because he's got a pool, a big house with a huge living room, the couch large enough for her entire family, and he always rents her fun horror movies filled with sex and cannibalism, even though she's only twelve. She likes going over to his house. He's got money and he's nice to her, buying her all the candy she wants. They even sleep over sometimes, Tita crashing on the larger than her family couch as Nymphomaniac's in Love screeches from the biggest TV she's ever seen, Twix and Big Hunk wrappers scattered across the coffee table, emptied cans of root beer stacked in triangles. Tita's sister's boyfriend is not a bad looking guy, not too tall, Tita's head reaching his broad shoulders. Tita's sister likes the haoles, always dating some kind of doctor, or some kind of chef, sometimes some tourist, other times some athlete, one time she flew to Chicago to marry some guy, but that didn't work out. When Tita's sister's boyfriend swims laps in his pool during the day, Tita admires his golden skin, his muscles, not too big, carving their way through the water. She pretends not to stare but he always smiles and makes her feel good.

Tita's sister invites him on a camping trip with their family, and he's excited, packing his Bronco with an inflatable mattress because he doesn't have a tent. He meets them down at the beach and Tita is happy to see him. He sneaks her a few Big Hunks, knowing her mother would be angry if she knew, and Tita smiles, happy he remembers her favorite candy bar. She watches him hang out with her father, awkwardly assisting with the bbq pit, trying not to get meat splatters on his nice beach clothes, and she smiles, and her sister notices, pinching her behind her arm, reminding Tita of her place. After dinner, she wanders away from her family talking story over the fire, her sister's boyfriend draping an arm around her sister, her dark hair, her dark face, nestled in his golden triangle. She drifts to the edge of the water, low tide uncovering pools shimmering in the moonlight, and Tita wishes she could just float in the dark, the water a cold black cocoon, stars prickling her skin, as she dreams of her dark hair, nestled in golden triangles.

Fishing for Akule

Tita sat on the edge of the seawall, the heat of the day burning her okole. She had made sure to sit far from the old uncle fishing for akule, his buckets and tackle surrounding his chair, so he wouldn't try to talk story with her, his pole relaxed in one hand, a beer hiding in a cozy in the other. She didn't need the hassle. The back of her calves scraped against the lava rock embedded concrete, the hot scattered sharpness feeling good. She regretted not bringing a bathing suit, the sea turtle, swimming around the truck tires that had come off the pier in one of the yearly storms, was definitely having a better time. Junior Boy wanted to join her but he knew better.

"You like go swim?"

"Nah."

He leaned against the wall, making sure he wasn't too close, waiting for her. She knew this. He watched tourists walk along the uneven sidewalk, waiting for one of them to trip so he could point it out to her, and they could laugh. He had called her last night and she hadn't pretended not to be home. They had talked about Mr. Nakatani and his computer he let them use sometimes to play games in his office in the woodworking shop. They had laughed at the Leisure Suit Larry game that made them take a quiz to prove they were old enough to play with stupid multiple-choice questions like *What wasn't part of Hawaii?* Fiji, and *Where's the …?*, beef. She had told him she was planning to go into town for the day, her mom dropping her off at the pier before going to work. He had hitched a ride early so he wouldn't miss her. She wasn't surprised to see him but it wasn't a date. He knew that.

"You ever think about getting away from here?"

"Sometimes. But like where I going go?"

She always thought about it, wondered about the freedom of escaping. Sometimes, she'd sneak into Mr. Nakatani's office late in the afternoon, when the final bell had rung and everyone had walked or caught their buses home. He didn't mind, he was constantly working in the shop, sawing, cleaning, sitting. She'd play her favorite game, Amnesia. No pictures like Larry. Just words. Her character would wake up in a hotel room, no memory, no clothes. She'd discover the mystery of his life in Manhattan, the woman he was engaged to, the man who wanted to murder him. The game a book she could play, almost as good as any Choose Your Own Adventure. She never told Junior Boy about these afternoons. They were hers.

"You could go anywhere you wanted."

"And leave Kona?"

He felt so alone when he was with her, even when they were sitting next to each other in Mr. Nakatani's office, laughing when they got Larry laid, or collecting items to solve puzzles in Space Quest, trying not to get sucked into the vacuum of space. The heat of her burning him. He never tried anything, even when she would lean back to laugh, her dark hair brushing against the hand he had placed behind her chair. She could solve all the puzzles so quickly, he felt useless offering her help. Yet, he kept going there during recess, lunch recess, after school, hoping to catch her playing.

"What's so great about this rock?"

"What's so great about anywhere else?"

She knew he wouldn't understand. She could see him here, sitting on this wall fishing for akule, waiting for some young girl to talk story with.

You Should Never
Eat Mangoes at Midnight

The day when I realized Sean Connery was in yellow face the heat had melted my ears away. The ears my grandmother had said were lucky. The gold piercings in them since I was six months old fell to the ground and I couldn't find them. No one in my family believed the heat was caused by the hole in the ozone or from solar radiation from unseasonable flares. My mother said my ears melted because I lost my luck and I needed to find it again.

The litany of accusations of what I probably did wrong consumed them. She kissed a boy. No, no, no, she kissed a girl. She didn't wash. Oh no, she washes too much. She never cleans under her bed. She is always helping the stupid neighbor boy with his math. She doesn't study hard enough. She always leaves the rice open. She reads too much. She always eats all the mangoes when we are sleeping. She lies.

No one else's ears had melted. The heat wasn't that bad they said as they fanned themselves and sipped on chilled oolong on our screened in lanai. Sharpen the knives my mother told me. Maybe if you do that well your ears will come back. You know, a knife if sharp enough, can cut you without sensation my father said to me.

For the Boy You Had a Crush on and Hoped Would Be under the Black Flap of Your Friend's Paku Paku

You spin out the hydrogen and helium, forming an accretion disk to surf along Saturn's icy rings as you flip through atomic numbers at the speed of an old dog trying to keep up with his leash puller, limping along to bubble gum, bubble gum in the dish, how many bubble gums do you wish, wishing that the table of elements was as periodic as the time you got blood on the bed and decided to leave it.

Relax Said the Nightman

Jen gets picked up for her babysitting job by Mr. Miller, *call me Ted*, in a silver sports car. It's the only time she ever babysits for the Millers. She runs her hands along the taupe leather of the interior, admiring the space-age dashboard.

When they leave her alone with Teddy, *put him to bed at 9, don't let him watch TV*, she puts Teddy on the beige sectional with a book and wanders over to the compact disc player Ted showed her how to use and she pulls out the Eagles from among the Beatles, the Smiths, the Dead Kennedys, Kansas, Boston, Chicago, takes out the shiny silver donut with her fingers holding it like a sandwich, remembering Ted telling her to be careful not to get smudges on the discs, and plops it down, pushing play and waiting for "Hotel California." She strokes the top of the stereo, another space-age machine of silver, leaving more smudges. She fingers the weird mask on the wall, all bristly hair, and staring eyes, the pupils open to the ecru paint behind it.

She goes into the kitchen and opens the fridge, *let Teddy have a snack if he gets hungry*, and sees an opened bottle of white wine, pops off the cork and takes a sip, burning her throat, pops the cork back on and puts it back. She lifts out a silver knife from another space-age contraption, dots running along its handle, and cuts a single strand of her hair with it. She pretends she's a pirate or a murderer, stabbing the air, her grip firm and true. She puts the knife back, sliding it swiftly into its sheath of metal, the ringing sound echoing around her, guitars shifting gears in the background as the tempo speeds up. She goes back to the fridge for another nip before getting the plate of cheese and crackers the Millers left for Teddy. She puts it on the sofa next to him but he doesn't seem interested so she gobbles a few of them before heading to the bathroom to pee.

Along the walls are pictures of the Millers without Teddy, sunny and blond and rich. Mrs. Miller is long and lean, always in white. Ted is long and muscled, not too much, and also in white and sometimes in khaki. She runs her hands along their bodies, white shimmering under her cheesy cracker fingers.

In the bathroom, *please use this one, it's for guests, we've locked our bedroom because Teddy likes to sleep in our bed and we are training him out of that*, she closes the door behind her. The white and beige and silver follow her. She lifts her shirt, her breasts bigger than they should be for her age, and pushes them against the mirror. She runs the water hot and puts her cheesy cracker fingers under it until they are scalded, rubbing them against her mirror cold skin.

Teddy doesn't fight her when she tells him to go to bed. She finishes his cheese and crackers, puts the dishes in the sink and has just a little more wine. She hits play again and listens until the Millers come home. Ted drives her back to the not so nice neighborhood, the windows down, the night air sweet and cool, he tips her an extra twenty for the night, pushing the money into her pocket before she can take it from him, his hard fingers digging into her skin.

in ache

she shuffles in flea market slippers too big for her flat walk-on-lava feet *you going grow into dem no worries* she veils her tears in a hand-me-down hasn't been quite white in a while mu'umu'u *you gotta wear dat to church so stop making any kine or you going get it* she feels adult in her first brand new blouse-not-shirt she buys from the Ben Franklin sale rack *you better wear em to school and take em off when you get home or else* she handwashes and hangs it oh so carefully fingers tracing edges of blue and white scallops *you stay stop daydreaming and finish da laundry* she shows it off once a week imaginary books on top of her head and her back model straight *you better stop wearing it your chichis stay getting too big* she buys heels with backs rubbing her skin raw blood dripping *you going need band aid but not going for help you* she pinches her toes hard to fit *you going get hamajang feet* a lesson she learns in ache scrubbing the dried mess of her mistakes the leather ruined forever

The Linebackers of Waikiki

We catch the bus to Waikiki on a Saturday, leaving our dormitories on the mountain behind. We want to tan and check out the hot tourists. The bus is cheap, only fifty cents. Our bags are packed full of coconut oil from Tahiti, blanket-sized beach towels, and sandwiches from the dining hall. There's no AC and the windows won't open. We are sweating in our shorts and tank tops, a rainbow of bikini straps tied around our necks, our already brown skin, glistening. We talk story about the hot young haoles we are going to see, seated two by two, inseparable. We transfer in Chinatown and can't sit together. An old lady blocks a row of seats, reading a porn magazine. We laugh behind our hands because we don't want to piss her off, but we all try to peek at the men and one woman doing the things we all know about but shouldn't. A man starts eyeing us up. We turn our bodies away from him, and he starts talking about our legs and how we could be linebackers and we get angry and want to get off the bus, but we don't because we don't know the bus routes well enough not to end up on the other side of the island. We put our headphones on, listening to Vanilla and his sexy voice, telling us to stop, collaborate and listen. The man gets angry at us for ignoring him, stands up and gets really close. We can feel his red eyes and even redder breath on our skin, the heat chills us. The old lady with the porn mag looks up at him, looks at us, and looks right back at her mag. The bus driver is too busy to notice until the guy's red scream shakes the whole bus, crashing down on us.

Or Better Yet

The aunties talk story around the food table, a gathering of tasteful floral patterns in an array of short mu'umu'u and billowy blouses. A bowl filled with poi, purple and thick, is placed in front of them, arms laden in golden bracelets, flicking at flies as they scramble for purchase on its rim. The uncles prick the aunties bubble with shouts for more beer as they brag about hunting wild boars with bows and throwing net for all the fish for the party. The aunties give them stink eye and yell for the kids to come and get some beer already, their tiny hands digging into the icy depths of the fishing coolers lining the wall, their tiny chilled fingers popping tops, uncles, creased by age and sun, teasing them for sips, dark arms around tiny shoulders, tiny hips, sparking laughter when tiny mouths spit it out, or better yet, keep it down. Tiny voices peep, excuse after excuse, the dark current of laughter pulling them under.

As All Titas Do

We watch her lay on the sand, self-conscious and bold, her dark hair fanned over her head. Soon the sun and sea will streak it blond and she will become a golden summer goddess, her brown skin worshipped by the surfers and boogie boarders, lining the waves. She doesn't quite know her fate yet, but we can see her future, shadowed in her creases, the boys and men she will welcome and the ones she won't. They will follow her, as they all do. And she will follow us, as all titas do. She will follow us into the dark after her first summer of glory.

To Ever Love One Girl

Cousin got whipped with the watering hose in the backyard so the neighbors couldn't see. Uncle wen catch her kissing one girl in town. He looped the hose and beat her over and over, slower than the sun beating her ehu hair into a matted mess on her scalp. I no get one lesbian for one daughter. You neva going see that girl again. You going to church. You going for pray. Each sentence a looped mark on her naked skin as he pulled her pants down and she tried to cover herself, crying and pleading. No please. I not one lesbian. I neva like kiss her. The heavy smack of that green snake shimmering in the sun, empty of water and engorged with hate, filled the yard as we cousins and sisters watched Uncle, his red browned skin and salty, peppery hair, his fisherman's arms, teach us that it's better to lie and to not be beaten and to suffer the drowning beneath the waves of beer and cigarette breathed fathers and uncles and cousins and brothers, our flesh torn by coral lined rocks as we tumble and toss, submitting to their little deaths, than to ever love one girl.

Want You

Your mother didn't want you. She threw you in a shopping cart and rolled you down the street to our house at the end of the cul de sac. Do you remember that house? The puke green paint and louvered windows, letting that dirty little Filipino boy next door peek at you girls in your rooms at night.

Your father didn't want you, either. He threw you in a cold shower every time you cried, your little body pummeled, your cries drowned out. He left you and your mother, high and dry, running off back to the mainland and his mainland life. You and your mother didn't deserve that haole, he was too good for you.

Your mother still doesn't want you. She visits when she needs money, running from one deadbeat boyfriend to another, waitressing under the table for cash and coke, serving up more than food. Do you remember the last time she came to pick you up? She wanted to take you to see your other brothers and sisters, but she couldn't afford to take you out to eat, so she borrowed fifty dollars. Where did you go? Oh, tuna and mayo sandwiches at a park in Kau? She never did pay it back.

You know we don't want you either but you are good to have around, good to clean our rooms, and wash our clothes, good to make us look good at school and in public, our trophy child, our good little adopted girl.

Where the Ali'i Are Hidden

Tita jumps off the lava rocks. Her legs bent, her fingers pinching her nose closed. She is a bomb, cratering the water as she passes through. She swims to the surface, the reef fish carving the water around her. She paddles along the rough coastline, happy the tide is low so she can swim to her favorite cave. She imagines that this is where they buried the Ali'i of her family. Their bones wrapped in kapa and placed so far back that no one alive would know where to look. She rides the swells into the waiting dark. The mouth, an arc above her head. Inside the light from the sun can barely reach it. She knows she only has a little time before it's too dangerous for her to stay. She listens to the echoes of the water against the rock, sounding like the blood in her own head. She hums and the sound drowns in the constant pull and push of the ocean, the blood flowing in and out of her heart. The water rises around her as she slowly lifts to the ceiling. She can almost brush her fingers if she pops herself out of the water but she knows if she stays the water will hold her down under a ledge and drown her before she can escape. In this moment, she knows she is both alive and not. No one would know where she was and she would finally know where the Ali'i were hidden.

Doing the Laundry

the laundry room of the apartment you lived in when you were four, you were so tiny, in your cute little jeans, lined with purple roses your mother let you have from the Ben Franklin, your cute matching purple T-shirt making you smile as you played in the driveway with your Chinese jacks because you were by yourself with no one to play with until one of the neighbor boys, so tall he blocked the sun, a halo around his blond head casting a shadow over the multi-colored rings arrayed before you, said hi and asked if you wanted to play and you were so happy not to be alone, and you went willingly with him into the laundry room, and he ran his hand along your flowers, and you knew, you knew, you knew something wasn't right, but you were frozen, your tiny body, your little hands, your purple flowers dropping to the ground

your mother strips all the bedding from all the rooms, all of your clothes, all of your sisters' clothes, fills garbage bags, drives downtown to Hele Mai Laundromat, drags you with her to help, it's your fault after all, you brought home the ukus, your shining brown hair will be washed in kerosene, washed in bleach, washed in detergent, because lice shampoo is too expensive, you will have your hair chopped short, you will have your scalp rubbed raw, you will have your hair torn out as your mother pulls out every egg she can find, her anger fueled by this, you will have to put all of the dirty uku laundry in the big washers, run the water hot, put in the detergent and the bleach while your mother scolds you from the side, yelling at you for getting dirty ukus from those dirty kids, you will not cry in the laundromat, you will not cry in the laundromat, you will not cry in the laundromat

you needed a dress for church and you knew your roommate had done her laundry, you were the bad roommate, borrowing money and clothes and food, no door between your rooms, and she must have hated you so much, but you thought she would never notice, you were so poor you barely had enough money from the scholarship you were on and you figured she wouldn't mind helping you out now and again, which turned out to be always, and you needed a dress for church so you found the black one you always borrowed from the school dormitory's laundry room and put it on, but you didn't borrow your roommate's dress, did you, you borrowed your dorm mother's dress, and that's stealing now, isn't it, but you were only borrowing, and now you have detention, and now you have to stay at your auntie's house but you don't care and you don't say sorry because your auntie has a pool and lets you eat whatever you want and you are just fine where you are

To Be Their Good Little Hawaiian

Tita wants jazz lessons not hula. She doesn't want to be that Hawaiian. She wants to stay home and study math and science. She doesn't want to babysit, clean, cook, help the aunties at the baby luaus, weddings, birthdays, anniversaries, graduations. She wants to hide in a corner and read a book. She doesn't want to be found by drunk uncles or cousins, asking for kisses or hugs or songs or dances. Tita wants to fly away as soon as she can. She doesn't want to be their good little Hawaiian.

Sacrament

Pua shifts in the pew as the water and bread are passed out by the chosen boys, her mu'umu'u scratchy and stiff against her skin. She wonders if it will be white or wheat bread. Her mother pinches her in the back of her arm so no one can see as the bishop drones on about stuff she should be paying attention to but doesn't want to, a whispered warning, hot in her ears *no shame me,* nails digging, pulling tears from her eyes *no make me take you to da car,* she sits still, her mother's fingers releasing with a last *no make me do dat again, girl,* her mother's eyes fire, a smile wide across her face as she checks to make sure no one heard her. Pua knows no one cares. She's sure all the other kids' arms are scratched black and blue too, their brown skin hiding all sins. The bread and water come to her row, her brother so proud in his aloha shirt and slacks, holding the tray and walking down the row. She hopes he drops it before he gets to her so he's the one who gets it and not her. He stops in front of their mother, her smile reaching her eyes. Carefully she lifts the piece of wheat bread and places it in her wide mouth, her lips close as she chews and swallows. Her fingers curve around one of the tiny little cups filled with water, her nails flashing red, lifting it slowly to her lips and sips it slow, savoring the moment, before placing the empty cup back. Her brother moves to her, his smile matching their mother's and Pua prays as she chooses her piece of brown bread, her mother's eyes hard on her.

The Opihi Shell Necklace
Hidden in My Mother's Closet

There are boxes of spam, corned beef, Vienna sausages, ramen stacked on the left in my mother's closet, bought with coupons and rainchecks. There are shoes in all the shades of taupe to match the nude nylons that don't match her skin, lined along the back wall. There are Harlequin and Silhouette romances on the shelf, rows upon rows, two or three deep, whose hues don't match hers either. There are dresses and slacks and blouses, smart and chic and ruffled, hanging from the good hangers.

I know there are hidden spaces in my mother's closet I can't reach. I know there are things I am not allowed to see. I know there are secrets. They whisper to me at night and I dream of grandma's opihi shell necklace, the one she was supposed to be buried with, glowing white on my dark skin, the ocean calling me home.

Kona Boy Made Good

There's a picture of me somewhere, wearing a space suit. My little brown bob, grown out from the last time I got ukus, dusting the metal ring around the neck hole. I couldn't believe how heavy it was, my arms and legs swimming in puffy whiteness. My hand shot up so fast when you asked who in the class wanted to try it on, my dreams of rocket ships and space, sparkling around me. I didn't know who you were then even though I had visited your parents' general store in Kealakekua after every coffee picking day, my back sore from carrying a basket of coffee beans around my waist all day. No matter how fast I picked or how many baskets I filled, I was never fast enough, or skillful enough, each hundred-pound bag filled by my parents, extra money for school shopping and Christmas presents. Maybe you picked coffee too? Maybe you were never chastised because your best was good enough to get you out of Kona and into space. On the day you died, I cried. In that moment, when the Challenger exploded, I saw the end of all of our dreams, Kona boy made good. And I remembered the kindness of your parents giving me a free cup of vanilla ice cream and a bag of freshly fried kettle chips, my face sweaty, my hands sticky with sap.

Oceans under Threat
Like Never Before

Tita reads the headline from today's paper. We wonder about what that means for us. It's hard enough just surviving here, our parents working all the time, our family living in a house they built subsidized by Hawaiian Home Lands, the land ours for only ninety-nine years. Nothing ours. Not really. Tita thinks it will mean all those golf courses will have to go and probably all of the hotels, too. There would still be beaches they just wouldn't have any sand. Not that sand matters to us. Most beaches on our island are lava rock anyway. We imagine swimming down Ali'i Drive, jumping off the big banyan trees into the waves. Maybe the whales won't come or they will come earlier or later, who knows. Maybe daddy and the uncles won't be able to go fishing any more, with no harbors to keep their boats. We imagine fishing from the top of Moku'aikaua Church, the steeple, the tallest point in town, casting our bamboo poles into the new coral reef growing on its rock-sided walls. We imagine tide pools forming in parking lots of abandoned hotels, wana finding purchase in the cracked asphalt, their black spines undulating in their new homes, sea cucumbers nestled along the yellow lines of the parking stalls, their colors camouflaged. We imagine our house on the mountain, finally a beach house, the ocean waves rolling in to welcome us home.

Sweet Water

Lani dreams of sweet water. The kind that drips off leaves onto your tongue in the rainforest. The kind that leaves your skin clean. The kind that waters your garden, leaves glistening in wet, and clears the dust from your eyes. Lani wakes to dryness. The kind that swells your tongue in your parched mouth. The kind that cracks your skin bloody. The kind that shrivels your garden and gathers dust in the corners of your eyes. She rubs the grit away, scratching her thin skin raw.

She licks the blood from her knuckles, salt she doesn't want to lose. Lani crawls from her mat in the corner of the coffee shack she shares with the husk of her mother's memories. She's so careful. She doesn't want to upset them, each layer perfectly preserving a giggle held in at a funeral, a waft of perfume from a night out with a first boyfriend, the taste of the first guava stolen from a neighbor's tree, the opening guitar lick of a concert snuck out to, wearing a best friend's leather jacket, the sound, a deep-down tingle, spreading out from clove-stained fingers. Lani carefully steps around these memories, holding her breath, so tempted to take each one of them in, quenching her thirst.

She doesn't lick the blood from her knuckles, saving her precious fluids. Lani picks herself up from the cot in the corner of the shed she shares with the husk of her mother's memories. She's not careful as she shakes her hands over each layer, drops blooming red in the sepia tones of waves carved into submission on the first surfboard, the ukulele played in front of a fire under a starry sky, the taste of tequila, burning an eager throat. Lani stomps around these memories, breathing them in, quenching her thirst.

She wipes the blood onto her shirt, adding to the clotted stains. Lani rolls over on her little bed, picked out special for her. She stares at the husk of her mother's memories, rocking in the acrid breeze. She can see the layers of birthday cakes and candles blown, butterfly kisses over a sleepy face, bedtime stories and cuddles under a sea of dolphins and whales and jellyfish, swimming above their heads. Lani drifts through these memories, soaking them in, quenching her thirst.

Or Else

The scream pierces the surrounding damp. Kainoa drops to the ground, trying to guess where it came from, his sweat-stained tank clinging to his wiry frame. He has been hiking through the rainforests, every day this week, searching the towering trees for maile leaves, the voices of his mother and the aunties, *eh boy, we need maile for the luau, your sistah stay getting married, you no like for us for be shame*, needling.

Another scream echoes through the valley. He slows, still scanning the trees around him for the precious vines, worried his family will be upset if he returns without them, *you bettah come back with plenty, or else Kai Boy*, he's not too old for dirty lickins, according to his father.

The next scream is so close he jumps when he hears it, almost slipping on the muddied red dirt, soaked from the morning rains. *What you stay scared for*, his father asks in his head, a fist always hovering. He tries to breathe, walking around another empty tree, his heart pumping. When the scream hits again, a glory of green greets him. A beautiful trail of maile vines, perfect for his sister's wedding, cradles the body of the largest boar he has ever seen, its sides scored with scars, its eyes wild, its mouth a blood froth, its leg, clamped, bone cracked in an illegal ring of teeth. When the next scream comes, he answers in reply, throwing his head back, eyes wet and wide.

We No Get Slopes

"I like go cruise up Mauna Kea. You like go tomorrow?" she says. I hear her breathe in quickly, worrying, "When snow."

"Who going take us? We no get one truck." I feel the sweat from my ear and hand slick the cordless handset. There's no fan in my room.

"We can ask Junior for take us."

"Then we going have to invite Yuki or she going think we trying for steal her man." I hunch forward on my bed, thinking about being cold because I'd probably have to sit in the back of the truck.

"Who like even try fo' steal Junior?"

"Fo' real." I lay back and laugh into the receiver.

Junior picks us up from my house. He knows where I live. I don't think Tania notices. Yuki got mad at us because she had to stay home to babysit and Junior still decided to take us anyway. Tania hops in first. She straddles the gear shift. I am more than sure that Junior doesn't mind her long leg against his. I step up into his cab and slam the door. He has woofers behind the seat and Black Uhuru pushes against our backs.

We leave Kailua behind and drive towards Waimea, turning onto Saddle Road. I stare at the rolling fields of ranch land before Mauna Kea and Mauna Loa come into view on either side of us. It's the quickest way to Hilo and the only way to Mauna Kea. There are way too many accidents and late-night-lady-in-white-you-better-not-have-pork-in-your-car Pele sightings for my taste, but I love Mauna Kea. When I was in the fifth grade, Ellison Onizuka visited my school, and I got to try on an actual spacesuit. I used to think it was so cool that he grew up in Kona. It made me believe that anyone could go to space. The closest I could hope to get to space now is flying in a plane, or maybe looking at it through a telescope.

Junior switches to Shabba Ranks as we drive past a campsite with log cabins and bbq pits. The music has been just a little too loud to talk, which is fine with me. When Mr. Loverman comes on, I glance past Tania, singing along, and over at him. He's smiling. I roll my eyes as we pass Pohakuloa, the army training base. It's all long huts and military trucks. It's quiet. No one is training this week. That's how Onizuka got into space. The military. Who wants that? I don't see Junior joining. Then again, he isn't Onizuka smart even though his family is Japanese. We turn on to the road to go to the summit. It's smooth until we hit the visitor's center. We stop in the parking lot and Junior gets out to turn his wheels to four-wheel drive.

"You like go to the visitor's center?" he asks Tania.

"Nah. It's just for tourists," she says. I just look at the side mirror's reflection of the road we came up, seeing the red brown slopes of Mauna Loa in the distance.

Luckily, the mountain isn't closed today because of the wind. The road is long and carves its way up the mountain, the gravel slides under the tires. We can't see the white bubble domes of the telescopes yet, but there was the wreck of a white rental car that had rolled down part of the mountain. "Stupid tourists." I say. They shouldn't have driven up here in that. We don't hit snow until we almost reach the top. The telescopes prick the sky, scattered across the snowy peak. The sun is already heading towards the horizon. A few clouds pass below. We park along the side of the road. There isn't a place for any of us to park up here. With the stereo off, we hear nothing when we get out of the truck.

"We should've come up early to get snow for take Hapuna," Junior says. I remember my hanabata days, when I was little, and my family would drive up here to shovel the snow and take it down to the beach for shave ice and snowball fights.

"I neva like go beach," Tania says.

"You guys know anybody who stay work up here?" I ask.

"Only get haoles. What locals can afford for go school and work up here?" Junior says as he leans against his truck next to Tania.

She nods her head. "I mean what local like work up here anyway? Stay cold and get better money down at the resorts. You can make cash tips." Her parents work at the Kona Surf. She wants a job waiting tables there during the summer. My parents don't work at the hotels but their jobs aren't that great either. My father cooks at a restaurant and my mother is an accountant. I don't want to argue with Tania, so I walk out onto the snow. It's pure and clean away from the road. I don't have gloves but I pick some up and form a ball, throwing it as far down the slope as I can, seeing if I can hit the lava fields at the edge. I don't make it. My hands hurt from the cold and I rub them against my jeans.

"I wonder if anyone try for ski up here?" I ask.

"If they do, they going end up in the rocks like that rental car." Junior laughs.

"We no get slopes," Tania agrees with him.

I wonder if the people in the telescopes came outside and played in the snow. They are probably too smart to do anything so silly. Junior picks up some snow and throws it at Tania. She shrieks and pretends to run away. I fall back in the snow, waiting for the sun to go down, so I can watch it set in the clouds on the horizon and for the stars to appear.

And Nothing Else to Do

"You like go cruise?" our boyfriends ask us on a Friday night, their heavy voices, weighing down the cordless phone in our hands. "We can meet everyone in the Sack 'n Save parking lot bumbai, drink some steinies. I even get some wine coolers for you." Their dark molasses voices, oozing through the ether.

Like every other night, we are sweetened and plumped, convinced to endlessly circle our little town, the lights of shops, restaurants, hotels sparkling the strip of Ali'i Drive, windows down, the cool sea breeze, salt-filled, saturating our skin in time to the bass kicking our bony depths from the trunk of their souped-up Japanese imports.

They pick us up, their cars shining under the sodium glow of the streetlight. Our skirts are short, our midriffs showing, hair long and curly, eyes lined, lashes full, ready for a night on a town much bigger than this one. A steady beat reaches our toes and travels up our spines. "You one honey tonight." They say this every time.

We know this routine will continue, like clockwork, the phone calling, the drinking in parking lots, the racing on mountain roads, the fucking in the driver's seat, the steering wheel hard against our backs because there is nowhere else to go.

Once upon a Time in Hawai'i

We glide to the boats on silent waves. Our paddles slicing through the waters. Our war canoes hidden in the darkness of a new moon. We are grateful for it. The Kahuna said their visions told them this was the night. We sweep around the outside of the bay so that they can't see us. We make sure to hide in the darkness. We climb up the anchor lines, keeping our canoes close, pieces of kapa along our hulls to keep them from making a sound. We have knives made of wood and shark teeth, their hilts gripped tightly in our mouths. We will kill all the men we see, throwing their bodies overboard, to be put in the canoes. We are shadows. We catch a man leaning against a rail. We slice his throat and throw him over for our brothers below. Another man is at the top of a long pole we climb as easily as a coconut tree, our blade almost removing his head from its stem. We have to leave him there, to honor him later.

The Kahuna tell us that the men in the rooms below will help us. They are useful. We are confused by what we see but we know what rooms are, what floors are, what sails are, these are not new to us. We had prepared ourselves for the strange way of things aboard their boat. We are not shocked when we can't open doors by pushing on them. We twist cold protrusions and they open. We are lucky and we thank Ku. The men are sleeping and we tie them up with the rope we have slung around our bodies. We don't want them to cry or shout so we put kapa in their mouths and we carry them easily on our shoulders. They weigh as much as children to us. We gather all of the living men on the top floors of their boats. Their eyes blaze at us but we know they will be grateful for their lives. Their boats are ours. The rest of their crews are on shore sleeping off their dinner and awa. We had made sure their food was seasoned with calming herbs to let them sleep deep, making sure they wouldn't wake up in the night during our raid. The men we have captured try to fight us. They are lucky we are so gentle with them. The Kahuna tell us to set them in the longhouse with the other men when we return. We burn more herbs inside the longhouse to keep the new ones calm as well.

The Kahuna tell us to bring out the one we believed to be Lono, their leader. We walk among the sleeping and drugged bodies and lift him up. His face filled with troubled dreams. Maybe he knows what is to come. Maybe not. We lay him before the Kahuna, gathered here for this moment. They talk among themselves, choosing one of us, asking me to step forward. You will take his life, and in doing so, capture his mana as your own, they tell me. I nod and kneel, readying my blade. His eyes flutter open as shark teeth slice through his neck, the blood spraying across the sand. In that moment, the world shifts and I know there's more to come.

They Would Have Told You

They would have told you not to go to that party. Bowls filled with candy and condoms. Tequila. Vodka. Rum. Bottles lining the counter. You and your friend, hiking across a closed golf course because the security guard wouldn't let any of you into the condo's parking lot. You would have been home studying US History for the summer school class you had decided to take to get ahead for college.

They would have told you not to drink all of that tequila, your tiny black tank dress barely covering your ass, your hair wild and free, the older girls, jealous of your body, no fat, no exercise, no care. They tell you that you will miss this when you are older; you laugh and keep drinking, stuffing your face with Hostess Ding Dongs from the freezer.

You know they would have told you not to go into the jacuzzi bathtub with that one boy and then in the shower, killing all of the hot water for the condo, after you went down to the beach with another boy and told him no because you were on your period even though you wanted to say yes, the tequila not quite making its mark yet.

They would have told you not to get the knife from the kitchen when you heard your friend scream, a mirror shattering, glass covering the bathroom floor, an angry punch not landing on its intended target.

They would have told you not to let the tequila spark the fuel of rage buried in you from recognizing the same glass shattering in your own life, punches always landing on their targets.

They would have told you not to plunge that knife into the wall next to his head, almost nicking his ear, as you see your friend crying, curled up in a ball, her hands covering her face, blood pouring from between her fingers.

A Primo Place to Stay

Turkeys screech on the oil-stained concrete driveway. She watches them through the louvered glass windows of the living room, strutting back and forth over greasy rainbows as she sprawls on the couch, her right leg draped over the top, calf grooved with curved indentions of rattan. She hopes the neighborhood dogs won't scare them off, or some asshole driving a truck too fast along the road. She likes the idea of wild turkeys wandering around the rainforest behind her house with their red wattles dangling on plump chests, pecking their way through the ferny undergrowth. She'd told other students on the mainland about them, but no one had known about the turkeys. They like to eat the fallen avocados from the tree next to the driveway. She doesn't blame them. They are delicious. Really, what kind of person would bring a turkey here and release it? She'd heard stories of pythons curled up near tiny streams, Jackson chameleons cruising tree branches, flocks of parrots buzzing people's houses. Turkeys? The idea of someone, or multiple someones, bringing in a turkey as a pet or as food and then thinking hey let's just let them go and see what happens makes her smile and cringe at the same time. She'd once found a polaroid she'd never seen before in her sister's photo album. She was small, sitting on the hood of a white sports car at night, holding a baby cougar, the dark sepia bleeding in from the white edges. If someone could bring in something that dangerous, then a turkey wouldn't even be a big deal.

She listens to their squabbling as the breeze raises tiny bumps along her exposed arms. She can smell the afternoon rain coming. Its green, wet scent nags her to take the clothes off the line. Instead, the sounds and smells drive her deeper into the hard, bird-of-paradise patterned cushions, the rattan creaking under her. She hates it. Hates its cheesy, mocking aloha print, reminding her of mu'umu'u worn for weddings, funerals, May Day celebrations, long, stiff material scratching her skin. The rattan furniture was for company, her parents insisted, but she likes the breeze that passes through the room. She stares at the palm leaf fan above her, dusty webs clinging to its wide bamboo fronds. The whole room makes her think of a hotel. Not a nice hotel like in Waikoloa, where the rich tourists stay, but an old hotel like Uncle Billy's in Kona with worn carpets, faded drapes, and chipped furniture, remembering better days when Kona was just a small fishing village and the hotel was a primo place to stay. They used to stay there for family reunions when rooms were cheaper. Now, they just have reunions at Old A's in one of the pavilions or camp down Napo'opo'o. Going to reunions always meant work, cooking, cleaning, babysitting. People she didn't like talking to her about things she didn't care about. When she was younger, she always felt like she had to please everyone. Now, she counts the days when she can just be away from them again.

She forces herself to roll off the couch onto the ceramic tiled floor. The rattan bites into her side while the grout between the beige tiles presses into the edge of her knee. They are almost too cold to touch. She pushes up, each of her hands spread wide, fingers soothed and repelled by the chill, and gets to her feet. They don't feel the cold as much as her hands. Years of walking barefoot on smooth lava rocks to jump into the ocean had widened and hardened them. She hates shoes with their heel bleeding blisters, toe cramping, make your feet look pretty in not quite Chinese foot binding ways. She walks through her mother's idea of a haole country kitchen, all white crockery and towels you can't use, and out the screen door. She puts on her slippahs and realizes she'd forgotten to grab a laundry basket. She hates laundry. She hates the sorting, hanging, folding. She hates that she can't use the dryer unless it rains all day. She kicks off her slippahs and slams open the screen door, hitting the side of the house with a loud bang. She hears a concert of squawks from the front of the house. She walks quickly through the kitchen and into the living room only to see that all the turkeys have vanished.

Coming Home

The streetlights are puddles in ink as Kahea weaves her way home along the cracks in the sidewalk, their sodium orange glow weakly shining on the neighbors' mango, avocado, tangerine, plumeria trees. She's just gotten off the night shift at the Sack 'n Save with a few pau hana shots in the back with the stocking crew before they got to work unpacking pallets loaded with canned food from the mainland.

Her car had broken down and she didn't have enough to get it fixed, so she walked the two and a half miles to work and back home again. She loved the quiet of the road at night. During the day, the streets were lined, bumper to bumper, no space for all the people who lived on the island. She'd walk past open windows blasting reggae or bass so low it vibrated her toes, closed windows filled with icy coolness she envied, and lifted trucks where her head barely reached the door handle, her embarrassment of not having a car a high humming counterpoint in her stomach.

She hears a screen door slam open as she nears her parents' house, her head snapping towards the sound. It's the house across the street. Jake's house. She hadn't spoken to him since she came back in failure from her one semester at a mainland college, no money to pay the tuition, the scholarships she had worked so hard to get not enough to cover everything, her parents too poor to help. She had left for college without saying goodbye. She couldn't. He never understood her need to leave their island behind. Their last night together a mess of booze and sex and anger on a beach under these same damn stars, pinpricks of don't leave, stay, marry me, their gravity wells, a prison.

She is surprised to see Jake, his long frame throwing its shadow against her. She won't make it to her own screen door before he gets to her, so she stands her ground. He goes to hug her and she pushes him away. His hair is shorn short. His eyes sunken.

"Kahea. I wen miss you."

"I know." She steps away from him.

"You neva say goodbye. You neva tell me you wen come back home."

"Why? Why I need for do any of that?"

"Cuz I love you."

"You don't even know what that means."

"You know I wen join up?" She shakes her head, not wanting to hear it. "I stay home from boot camp."

"So what?"

"Don't you love me?"

She breathes in the heavy scents of the yards around her, the heat of the day cooling, releasing life into the darkness.

"No." She turns away into the light of her parents' porch.

"I'm sorry," he says into the empty space she's left behind.

Giving All the Aloha

Shannon needs a ride to work but her stupid boyfriend has left her with no car and no money for a taxi. She wishes she could take a bus but there's only one on the entire island and it just goes in a circle. She thinks hard about walking, but it would take her almost two hours on the side of the road with no sidewalks, watching tourists driving past, honking and laughing at her. She hates her job. Working the counter at a pizza shop sucks, the boss always trying to grab her ass, brushing against her chest as he walks past her at the cash register, but she puts up with his shit because he pays her cash under the table, no taxes, no social security, and she gets to keep all the tips in the jar next to the register. Most of the time the customers are tourists staying at the resorts and condos along the seashore, so she smiles wide, her brown skin against her shark white teeth, giving all the aloha she can for that fiver in the tip jar. Most of the time it's the change, but every once in a while, she scores big time and they can splurge with their dealer, loading up on a few different varieties. On those days, she remembers to bring home a couple of pizzas, white for her and pep for him, hoping he remembers to pick her up without her having to beep him. She thinks about calling in but takes a hit from the bong in front of her to chill out and wishes she could just fly to work, over the sunburned heads of tourists in their rented convertible Mustangs, the beach bums surfing their days away, her boyfriend probably one of them.

Believe We Are Magic

1980

She pretends to skate around the living room. Bobby-pinned to her dark hair are a rainbow of used plastic ribbons she took from the special birthday and Christmas box her mother keeps in the closet. She imagines them cascading down her back, the breeze blowing them gently behind her as she swirls in her bare feet on the golden area rug. She wants pale flowing hair and real roller skates as she sings *you have to believe we are magic*, wishing she were a muse and not a little girl.

1984

She stares hard at the man who is not a woman but wears makeup like he is. She knows there is something special about him. He rides a motorcycle, wears puffy sleeves and tight pants, his eyes lined, his lips full. He's not a mahu as her mother would call him, and she wants to go crazy just like he sings, wear purple and white and pile up her curly hair to cascade down around her, but she doesn't know how, and she's too afraid to ask.

1988

She doesn't tell anyone how much she likes the guy who is the blue alien, his golden skin and dark-lashed eyes so different from the boys at school. She sings *'cause I'm a blonde* even though she isn't, her boobs bigger than everyone else's. She shakes her cosmic thing. She learned how from the hula and Tahitian lessons her mother made her take even though she insisted she didn't want them.

1992

She is drawn to the lounge singer pretending to be a nun in order to hide from her mobster boyfriend. She isn't someone her mother would think is beautiful but she is enchanted by her otherworldliness. She remembers listening to her mother's albums, her body surrounded by the halo of the living room rug, singing *I will follow him*, blending her voice to the one on the stereo. Now, she imagines all of these different voices and hands and bodies entwined, worshipping, *there is not a man today who could take me away* and they'd all chorus together, finally believing she is magic.

Why I Only Dated White Guys
Growing Up

you bettah not bring one popolo home my mother told me when I thought Michael Jackson was cute *eh, why for you wen kiss your cousin at your auntie's wedding* my mother told me when my sister caught me at first base and told on me *your cousin wen get lickins with the hose because her fada wen catch her with one girl* my mother warned me *you bettah off with one haole they get money* my mother instructed me

Crush

We climb the roof of the haunted dormitory. You want a smoke without getting caught, and I try to scramble up behind you, envying your long legs as they stretch to reach the overhang from the wall we scaled to reach it, my own heaviness a struggle.

We walk to the side facing the valley, the tiles shifting under our feet. There's no one else crazy enough to do this, so we are safe. We dangle over the edge, the lights of the houses below, the lights of the stars above, the lights of your cigarette and lighter are shining in the hush around me.

I imagine the fuck-me red lipstick, as you call it, a swirling invitation across your lips that you offered to me but I refused even though I wanted it on me. I imagine your eyes, catlined black, carefully drawn on in the mirror of your locker above mine. I have been the dark shadow you don't want to shake.

You casually flick your ash with a cool I can never master. "We should have brought some booze." I shrug and you turn away.

I can smell the mix of your shampoo and perfume and the tobacco. I try to breathe deeply without you noticing but you do and turn back, ash floating towards the depths.

"You can kiss me if you want."

I don't and you crush your cigarette against my heart and scroll Fat Slut in fuck-me red across my locker the next day.

A girl

A girl sits, waiting. She reaches above her head for a girl. A girl to pluck from the tree of girls. The tree is full and ripe, the perfect tree for a girl. A girl wishes to taste the fruits. The fruits taste of a girl. A girl is sweet, salty, fiery, free. Fire fills a girl every day. A girl jumps up, stops waiting. Picks a girl. A girl tears into fiery flesh. A girl tastes the salt of blood. A girl smiles. A girl cries. The tree shudders under the weight of a girl. A girl is shuddered free. A girl falls for another girl to pluck. To pluck a girl. A girl is not ripe now but rancid. Rancid girls are no longer a girl. A girl is shocked. A girl is surprised. A girl shakes the tree again for a girl. Find a girl. Kiss a girl. Hold a girl. A girl holds a girl. A girl waits no longer.

Another Night on da Kona Pier

They pulled into the pier, driving past the huge old banyan tree in front of the hotel, orange streetlights turning roots, trunk, and branches into tentacles that reached for ground and sky. They headed slowly towards the end, parking near their friends' cars. She looked out at the horizon framed in the passenger side window, stars marking where the ocean stopped and they began. The bass, pulsing from the trunk of Jake's Mazda, buzzed the glass. He'd been really into gangsta rap lately, playing a lot of NWA. She would have preferred some Bob, so they could chill, but she didn't have the car or the stereo to compete, so she was left to deal with what he decided was cool. She didn't have to listen to the words to enjoy the beat at least. She wondered if she should have hung out with the surfers down at Pine Trees, but she had promised Kim that they would cruise town tonight and meet up with Jake and his friends.

They were dressed for a night out at a club that didn't exist, short skirts and high heels, dark eyes and red lips. She'd brought a bottle of tequila filled with li hing mui seeds. She'd scored it off her cousin, who had the hook up with one of his bosses at work. She passed it around for everyone to take a swig, the little red seeds adding a sweet and sour tang to the fiery liquid. She was long past the days of wine coolers, sixth grade slumber parties filled with horror movies and fuzzy navels. She'd had a brush with some 151 during a crazy weekend in Waikiki and she didn't want a repeat of that. She liked having her own bottle to carry around. She could sip or shoot whenever she felt like it, and at the end, she could break the bottle open and eat all the seeds soaked with tequila.

"This is so ono, Lani!" Tanya said. "I can't believe it."

"Yeah, I wen get the idea from my auntie wen she wen make em with vodka. It makes it so sweet."

The guys passed up the tequila. They already had their green bottles in hand, and Jake replied, "Garans, beah before licka eva sicka, so no worries, we going be fine with our steinies." She laughed in her head. She didn't want to piss him off. She thought that rhyme was so stupid. If they couldn't handle their liquor, then they were a total waste of her time. She didn't always like hanging out with Jake and his friends. They were all out of high school and working. Jake was at a car stereo place. They always had booze and smokes so she didn't have to buy anything for herself if she didn't want to. She'd had sex with him once. She was drunk and horny, and he kept checking her out. She probably shouldn't have done it. She had known Kim liked him. She didn't understand why. He was kinda stupid and not very cute, but to each his own. She bummed a menthol off of him and leaned against his car, her body vibrating. She watched the lights of the town shimmer on the water, long lines of red, orange, yellow, the tip of her cigarette, a fiery reflection. She ashed it, the night trades pulling the graying ember towards the glass-bottom boat moored to the pier.

"May I have drag, Jake? I don't need a whole one." Kim smiled at him. He passed it to her and she put the cigarette to her red lips, not really inhaling. She'd be so pissed if some chick put lipstick all over her cigarette, but when she looked at Jake taking it back from Kim, he hadn't seemed to mind.

"Ho brah, I wen drink one whole case last night. I was so wasted." Tony bragged to Jake. "I was going call you for come hang out my house but I figure you was busy with your honeys." Tony looked over at her. She rolled her eyes. He just lost out tonight. Too bad. He at least had a car. She checked out the rest of the guys. Not much there. Jen and Tanya were draped all over Billy's Camaro. She tipped the tequila back, sweet warmth spreading to her toes, and pushed herself away from the constant thumping to walk over to them. They had gotten a couple of beers from the guys, but she passed them her tequila and they gratefully took a few sips.

"So, Lani, how come you stay in Kona?" Billy asked.

"She's home for the three-day weekend," Tanya answered as she moved closer to him.

"Oh yeah? You no have to stay at school?" They all knew she was going to Kam School on Oahu but they always asked these stupid questions.

"Nah. They close the school, so we gotta go home."

"So what? You going college?" He persisted as he moved towards her. Shit. She could see that Tanya was getting worried.

"Maybe." She moved to the other side of the car, where Jen was hanging with Tony. "You like some more, Jen?"

"Nah, I got a good buzz now."

"How about you Tony?"

"You know what? Garans. I going try it." She smiled at him as she passed him the bottle.

"Chee hoo! That buggah is strong but ono. Thanks sistah."

"No worries. Let me know if you like try some more." She killed her cigarette on the ground.

"Hey, Jen. You want to take a walk?"

"Sure."

They walked along the edge of the pier, hearing the water lap against the huge truck tires tied along it. The lights from the hotel in the distance twinkled along its sloped walls, reminding her of dreams of skateboarding down and jumping off them into the ocean as a kid. "Do you think we will be stuck in the mud here for the rest of our lives?" She asked Jen as she thought about the guys working their shitty jobs every day and cruising town every night.

"Man, I don't want that. I'm going to college. I want to leave all this behind." They continued around to the other side of the pier, facing the ancient temple, a grass shack surrounded by tikis, their faces hidden in the shadows cast by the lights of the hotel's luau grounds behind it.

"I don't want to be trapped on this rock either." She wished she'd bummed another cigarette from Jake or gotten some cloves from Honolulu before flying home.

"Can I get another sip of your tequila?"

"Of course." She passed the bottle and watched the luau lights turn brown as Jen lifted it to her mouth. "You ever just wish you were already grown up and on the mainland living life?" Jen gave her back her bottle and nodded. They started walking towards the little beach in front of the King Kam, the lights of the luau grounds moved with the low tide surf coming into shore.

"I see the kids I go to school with and they are all rich haoles and I think you just wait until I am making lots of money and I don't have to be shame I'm on a scholarship," Jen replied. "At least you at Kam School and you can be with other Hawaiians."

"Yeah, but they try to make us as haole as possible."

"You gotta be able to pass as haole or you aren't going to make it."

They turned towards the old banyan tree, seeing the bars and restaurants still open across the street. They had passed other groups of people, parked, drinking and talking story. They got a few catcalls but they were used to it. They all probably thought the girls were too hai maka maka and they were probably right.

"Anything to get out of here."

The girls stopped in front of the banyan tree, its roots cracking and bending the sidewalk. They crossed the street to the seawall that stretched all the way to the palace. She imagined what the seawall would have looked like with the old torches her father had told her about, when the gas line had run under the wall and the torches would be lit every night at sunset for the tourists. She bet the tourists weren't too happy hearing all the locals hanging out in front of their hotel, having a good time, definitely not being good little Hawaiians.

They made it back to their group. Jen walked back to the Camaro and leaned on the trunk. She saw that Jake and Kim were hanging out. Jake was so much taller than Kim, but then again, a lot of guys were. Kim was short but cute. She didn't blame Jake. Kim was a nice girl. Jake had changed the music to some Gregory Isaacs. She smiled. At least it was reggae. She thought about going over to Jen but decided to walk back to the edge. She closed her eyes and swayed to the slow rhythms, Gregory's voice pouring over her. The smell of the ocean, the feel of the breeze on her skin, the slow, sexy tempo of Night Nurse, and the tequila worked their magic, carrying her away.

The Mongoose

The Mongoose took out a semi today according to the uncles and aunties. There was a blurry brown streak under the front wheel and the rig skipped over the edge of the embankment, taking out the guardrail, crushing all the trees and bushes in its path as it rolled down the slope, the attached container bursting, pallets loaded with toilet paper, fresh off the boat, trying to escape. No one saw how it happened but everyone knew it was The Mongoose.

You had to be careful on the roads. It was better to let a mongoose pass and possibly get a fender bender than to run it over and total your car and maybe yourself. Sometimes, after a few drinks, the aunties and uncles would talk about its origins. Some of the uncles thought it saw its parents die, killed by an unwary motorist, and, in its rage and sadness, became this immovable being. Some of the aunties thought it was just so tired of humanity that it liked to see how much chaos it could cause by hurtling its improbably strong body under any and all tires it could.

We liked to play mongoose roulette. We'd drive with the lights off on our dark mountain roads. It really wasn't much of a risk. They actually hunted during the day. We were more likely to fly off the edge of the road than hit a mongoose, let alone The Mongoose. We still liked the thought of testing our luck. We figured if we miss it or it missed us, it would probably be a good weekend, if not, what better way to go, we'd laugh to ourselves as we drank and smoked, parked along our dead-end streets.

Principles of Lust

He drives through the cobalt night, the stars glaring down as they fly across the sky, the glow from his dashboard a pale mimic. A mix of Gregorian chanting, synth beats and sexy French singing bleed pink from his speakers. He parks on a dark mountain, hiding you both, but the repeating music is an easy echo for the cops to find if they cared to, but they don't. You get out to look at the lights of the homes and the towns flowing away from you, reflecting the sky above, constellations of lives being lived. You start to dance as he gets out too. Watching. Waiting. You know why he drove here. You know why they all drive you here.

Out of Sync

I take a sip of the green bottle they hand me. I don't care what it is. The lights of Kona spread out before us. The music thumps in the cool mountain air. I tip back and finish it. They swear. I laugh. I toss it. I pull a tequila bottle from my backpack. I don't share. They swear. I laugh. The first sip is fire. I don't cough. The second lacquers my throat, easing me into them. My grip loosens and so does my tongue. I lick the rim of the bottle, the peppery flavor stinging. I lean against them, the bass line hooking me deeper. I don't relinquish my bottle, yet. I take a long slow swallow, my heart out of reggae sync. They take the bottle from my hand and pass it around. I don't care as I ride the rhythms of a different island far away.

All Wisdom Is Not Taught
in Your School

The white cotton mu'umu'u we have to wear for graduation, scratches and itches and strangles our necks, our arms, our wrists. We are enshrouded for the celebration. Our faces and hair, dark, medium, light, a rainbow of humanity, awaiting the next step of our sublimation. We sing praises to the past and sing hope for the future, but they are lies we taste, ash on our tongues. We have been indoctrinated in the very culture that wants nothing to do with us but we haven't learned that truth. Not just yet. We pray to a god that tried to change us to fit his image, our love our openness our welcome, converted to hate, selfishness, exclusion. We drift like ghosts across the stage, our ancestors, shadows hiding in the corners, telling us no, don't, free yourself, protest. The irony never crossing our minds as we exchange one white shackle for another.

the graduation party
you decided to skip

fishing coolers engorged with freshly bought beer, uncles smiling and laughing, stroking cigarettes and ukuleles, playing for aunties shoo shooing flies away from the buffet tables, laughing and yelling at kids screaming and tagging around the edges, your friends waiting and talking story, their necks laden with maile, ti leaf, flowers, fake and real, money, candy, yarn, their necks and chins hidden from each other, as you drive to the end of the world, throwing all the leis, including the money, into the pounding surf beneath you, wishing you could join them, escaping the promise of tomorrow

Stifling the Weeds

We lay recycled cardboard on the dirt of our little plots of land, a cheap way to block weeds from growing, organic, if the cardboard doesn't have anything poisonous hidden in its folds, ready to kill the life we are growing. We argue over dry taro, ulu, sweet potatoes. Our need for fresh produce of our own, a constant, fighting worms, snails, blights, diseases, brought from foreign lands. We till the dirt, red and fertile from ancient lava flows. We discuss growing wet taro for poi but we know that will take more water than we can afford, rain caught and stored not enough to flood even one crop. We gnaw fingernails and broken skin, our anxiety at surviving on our homeland a struggle. We share our ebts to gather groceries and necessities brought on shipping containers, grateful we even have land to work even if we can't earn enough money working at the resorts, restaurants, construction sites to pay for a single bedroom apartment, to keep a roof over our head, forcing us to camp next to the cardboard we pulled from dumpsters behind the Walmart.

the mongooses of Pahala

we run from the smell of burning cane, the heat following us as we join the rats we were brought here to kill, the sick sweetly smell clinging to our fur, the dried dirt puffing under our paws, claws scrabbling into the scrub brush and lava fields along the edges of the stalks, our lungs drowning in burnt sugar and we dream of fighting cobras and we dream of running free through forests damp, fields of rice, along holy rivers and we dream of a home we can never return to

Living on Stilts

Our houses stay on stilts but we no live near the ocean. Our daddies they wen tell us the lava rock no like foundations, so it stay better to build with the land. Wen Pele stay angry we barely feel it, her ami barely circling to our little volcano. She like Kilauea better anyway, probably get one boyfriend over there. Our mommies laugh wen we tell them. Mommies know the truth. Pele going go where she like and it's never about the boyfriends, that's just daddies being stupid. Our houses stay on stilts and one day Pele going knock em all down.

Be Careful What You Wish For

You wen collect da hair and fingernails he asks as his puffy white hair
dances in the ocean breeze and you answer *yeah, yeah I did, no worries*
but you worry *don't you no worries me if you never do it, you not going get
what you want* he scolds through broken teeth, his breath, rotting fish
and seaweed, *I stay know Tutu I wen get 'em* you insist *okay den put 'em
on the table* and you place upon the weathered picnic table in front of
him the long ehu strands and clipped slivers you stole from her brush
and wastebasket *you sure you like do this, you know going be permanent*
he grins wide, his tongue blacker than the night surrounding you *yes,
Tutu I stay sure, I stay need her* you plead and his milky eyes shine in the
moonless night *okay, Kawika* and Tutu pulls the pieces of your woman,
the woman who wants to leave you for another, and he weaves the
words of your ancestors, casting this simple spell for you, remembering
the days when he chanted for green fireballs to rain down on enemies,
for the cursing of the womb of a rival chief's woman, for blights cast
upon the taro fields of hated neighbors, and he pities you, knowing
you don't understand, and his lips spread, his dark maw working, the
money you already paid him burning a hole through the universe

The Day Captain Cook Missed Hawai'i

We were celebrating our harvest. Food had been gathered and prepared for weeks. Men had fished and filled our ponds. Taro roots, our brothers, had been harvested and made into poi. The leaves stewed or steamed in underground ovens with fish, pigs, chickens. New kapa had been made by the women of the ahupua'a as they shared news of their preparation through the mountains and valleys, the sound of their rhythmic pounding, a comfort. Men and women were dancing in praise of Lono, their hair shorn to make the necklaces woven with whale bone. We were listening to the history of our people, the elders singing and chanting with drums and ipu. We were thankful for another bountiful year. We were not at war. The Kahuna were praying and sacrificing. It was a sacred time for all. Some were forgiven for their crimes, free to leave the refuges around the island. We didn't know what we were missing.

Paradise

The lion died the day the circus arrived, the asphalt of the old airport steaming the hay in its tiny cage, the trade winds carrying a mix of salt and musk and decay from the beach nearby through our fishing village.

We were so eager to see him perform, top hats and whips, chairs and fiery hoops, under a candy cane striped tent, all the things we'd seen on tv, in movies, in Saturday morning cartoons.

Now, his spirit stalks our sea wall, weaving around the ghostly torchlights of our fake paradise past, his silent roar, echoing in the surf.

Kona Doesn't Want You to Visit

She's fine. She has enough people now. She could probably do with less. Her pier is filled to the brim with cruise liners dumping their passengers for the day, homeless locals and homeless not locals, glass-bottom boats to see the fishes, snorkeling cruises to see more fishes swimming under Cook's white obelisk, tourists staying at the hotel laying out on their little beach, an ancient temple's gods watching them. Her roads are filled with too many cars, one bus circles the island, her people spending hours to drive less than ten miles. Her shores are filled with golf courses and resorts her people treat themselves to when they aren't working at them. Her mountainsides are filled with coffee plantations her people can't afford to work at because it's cheaper to hire more not locals from other lands as oppressed as hers. Kona wants more than what she has now. She remembers the days when Ali'i walked her shores, breaking the ancient kapu, the queen eating bananas with her son. She wants revolution again.

Casting Nets

The sharp wind slices the stubble on Eddie's cheek as they take the boat further from the coastline, Kona and the rounded tip of Mauna Loa disappearing in the distance. They need to find the school of ahi. They know it's out there. There are only three of them this time. Eddie, his father, and uncle Nephi. They had to leave cousin Calvin behind because he just couldn't handle his beer, three silver cans down and he was fighting everyone around him. Nephi had charted the ahi's movement, predicting where they would go next for food, knowing how the waters flowed like streams, rivers, seas, in the vastness of the Pacific.

The waves swell higher than the captain's deck, his father commandeering the best seat on the boat, navigating by feel, his hands gripping the wheel. Eddie holds on to his seat underneath as the ocean threatens to cover them in uncompromising salt water. He feels like he will die, and secretly hopes that he will, a wife and several children waiting for him, always waiting for him. He misses the days when going fishing meant easy money, bumps of coke to keep him awake, tequila when the catch was in the hold. He wants to yell at his father and his uncle, scream why are we here when Nephi gives a holler and points to a dark cyclone underwater, the ahi swirling, a funnel of feeding.

The water fights their net as they cast and drag it as low as they can go, not wanting to spook the ahi in their frenzy. They time it, their distance allowed by the crane uncle Nephi had welded. They scoop them quickly, their silvery bodies straining against the net, their razor teeth slicing through the weave, through each other, almost through Eddie. He hurries, pulling in their catch, their blood mixing with the salt water on the deck. He dumps them into the hold, their bodies flashing in the darkness beneath him.

The Cannibalistic Sea Slug

Nudibranchs or Naked Gills live their entire life exposed, no shell to protect them.

One time, my mother tore off my yellow one-piece swimsuit because it was too sexy. My hips were too revealing. My crotch too suggestive. You are a whore, she said. I was eleven.

Nudibranchs get their colors from the food they eat, which helps with camouflage.

One time, my mother made me eat food from the trash because I had mistakenly thrown it away. I buried my tears, and swallowed every bite, not daring to hold my nose even though the smell could make me vomit, and she would make me eat that too. You are garbage, she said. I was eight.

Some nudibranch species are colorless.

One time, my mother washed my hair with bleach because I came home with lice. My skin burned, my hair dissolved. You are an animal, she said. I was six.

Nudibranchs can keep predators away with toxic secretions and stinging cells.

One time, I dreamed of running away and wrote it down. I wanted to tell my secrets to someone who would listen. I dreamed of saying no. I dreamed of fighting back. She found it and burned it in front of me. You aren't going anywhere, she said. I was thirteen.

Nudibranchs eat their own kind.

One time, my mother called me to tell me she was dying. I love you, she said. I was forty.

Tweezer

Your hair is going gray but you don't want to dye it yet. That would admit defeat. I part its darkness in uneven rows, with a comb, starting in the front and working my way to the back, hunting. Pull it out from the root, you instruct, but I can't get a good grip with my tiny hands and I break it, don't tell you, and I keep trying to find my targets. It's not fun but I have to do it, or else. You are seated in front of your makeshift vanity and I am standing on a stool because I am not quite tall enough but you don't care as my arms and legs hurt from the minutes that feel like hours.

You finally give in, and also decide to take me to get my eyebrows professionally done. The Brooke Shield's look is so out honey, the man at the beauty shop tuts at me. You smile in agreement under your shower cap of black. You didn't tell me that I would spend my mornings, my hands finally big enough, tweezing my own face, after this, but I do, and it's all hunting and trying to pull it out from the root and breaking and remembering your anger which is mine.

Later I will think about those days of searching and plucking and breaking the white hairs on your scalp, the veins, blue and red beneath my growing hands, as I move across my own face. Sometimes I think about those weekend afternoons and wish we had shared something more than this.

Fire and Sea

I laugh at your need to keep your knees covered, shorts too long, pants too short, colors muted and dark. At night, I unpeel you, uncovering hair grown along scars from childhood scrapes along coral, swirls in patterns of fronds, cerebellum, a reef of skin for me to swim over.

You mock my cravings for raw chili peppers, burning my lips with each seed, the oil, a glistening inferno on my tongue. At night, you pluck each tiny red body from the bush, run it along my skin, memories of taunts and screams, sugar, milk, bread, a conflagration never quenched.

This Is a Story about That Can of Tuna You Left on the Counter

Did you leave it for me to find? A trophy of your successful hunt through our bare pantry. Left for me to marvel at your ability to fend for yourself. Its jagged lid, torn away by the ancient ten cent can opener you bought at a garage sale, propped up by a crooked sliver you decided wasn't worth the manual labor to remove.

The spoon is where you left it too, the bowl half-buried in oil-soaked remains, the bent handle jutting out almost parallel to our marbled Formica counter, another cheap garage sale find. Why didn't you finish it? I had made rice. Then again, I like tuna on hot rice. Not you.

You could have put the whole can in the fridge like you've done before. The smell permeating the shells of eggs, the sides of condiments, the carton of milk so much so that I had to clean the entire thing on the one night I was free, wishing I was on a beach back home with no worries or cares.

Now, the smell blankets our small kitchen with no windows to open as I dump what's left into the over-filled trashcan you haven't emptied yet. I wash it out, bending and straightening the lid to pop it off, as you knew I would, placing the split pieces on the counter to dry.

Two Finger Poi

Tita doesn't know how to pound poi. She knows how it's done. She's seen it on fieldtrips to the city of refuge along with games played by her ancestors, throwing long wooden spears at banana trunks, rolling round stones through tiny posts, a not-checkers game played with white coral and black lava stones. She remembers the long stone, carved into a canoe-like shape, the poi pounder, a silhouette of a woman, hips wide. The taro, peeled and steamed, piled in a koa bowl.

The Tutu kneels, praying for the bounty, before putting one of the cooked and cooling taro onto the stone with one hand and wrapping his other around the neck of the pounder, a chant sounding across the ahupua'a, the pounding a rhythm communicating for all to hear, the gossip of the day. The people are working to prepare the feast. It is makahiki. The tutu works steadily, each taro pounded before a new one added, the fullness of each, flattened and thick, water added to thin it for the feast.

One finger, two finger, three finger poi, Tita thinks about how thick poi should be. She has always been a two finger girl even though she's supposed to use a spoon but if you have to twirl it more than two times than it's too thin, she tells her little sister. Her little sister is too young to care, she just uses her whole hand in her little bowl.

The bowls of poi are passed around as the people eat their fill of fish and pork and chicken all cooked in the underground oven, the steam and salt, creating moist, flaky, fall aparts, perfect for the sourness of the poi, its purple, a gorgeous contrast to the array of cooked white flesh.

The people are thankful to the tutu and the gods for their abundance, all work on hold until the end of the holiday.

Tita wants to make poi from scratch for her first Christmas with her husband, a steamer and blender helping her create her childhood. She has the taro shipped from Hawai'i. She knows it is worth it. She peels and steams and cuts, placing each chunk into her highspeed blender, careful to add just a little bit of water because she is still a two finger girl.

How to Care for the Giant Hawaiian in Your Life

Chapter 1: Feed her.

Actually, no don't feed her. She can feed herself. Just don't judge her if she wants to eat Spam. She can't help it.

Chapter 2: Water her.

She needs the ocean, but any river, lake, stream, pond, inflatable pool will do.

Chapter 3: Love her.

As she is, no more, no less, no matter how big or small or loud or quiet or how she slips into pidgin when she is angry or drunk or both.

Chapter 4: Touch her.

She wants hugs but not all the time, or every day, or only when you want it.

Chapter 5: Leave her be.

She doesn't need to be rescued and she doesn't need to rescue you. You are not Platonic selves split in two. You are individuals with their own damn baggage. Figure out your own shit first before trying to solve anyone else's, especially hers.

Chapter 6: Talk with her.

She is more than an avatar of what you think Hawai'i is. She is the end result of colonialism, imperialism, Mormonism, Protestantism, commercialism, tourism, and multi-generational traumas. She might open your eyes.

Chapter 7: Support her.

No matter what crazy diets, exercise plans, music lessons, writing workshops, art classes she obsesses over.

Chapter 8: Trust her.

She will always be there for you. She's loyal. Until you piss her off. Warning - Don't do that.

Chapter 9: Be worthy of her.

She's worth it. Work on yourself. Get your life together. Be equals. Be human. Or don't date, get into a relationship, and marry her. You have been warned but it's totally worth it. Trust me.

Shiriyaki Onsen

We drive into the mountains in a tiny rental car, dipping in and out of valleys, filled with the changing season. A night at a small ryokan away from our city awaiting us. We greet the obasan at the door, her hair short and curled, a brown apron over her sensible clothes. We put our shoes into cupboards, slipping our slippers on, carrying our luggage to the room we will share. We change, laughing and ready to relax, walking to the river. We pass bodies sprawled, our eyes wandering away. We gather in swimsuits, towels wrapped, hair tied up, hiding our not naked bodies.

We swim in a river filled with demon waters. The heat pooling around rocks as we sip bottles of chilled rice wine, a hint of sulfur tickling our noses. We float in a valley, colored and carved. The reminders of death, red, yellow, brown, drift down around us. We watch a cock-ringed peacock strut along the river's edge. The silver plumage nests in curled hair. We cup our giggles so as not to scare his display, the ice melt cooling our hot bodies.

We pull ourselves out of the water, our skin slick under our swimsuits and towels, and sit on the edge, river rocks digging into our flesh. The cooling air of the afternoon breeze through the valley sends goosebumps along our drying skin. Our feet dangle in the water, ripples spreading outwards and through each other. We settle back in the water to warm up again, our skin red from the waters, our cheeks flush from the wine, the peacock forgotten.

The Helicopter Pilot Who Decided to Preach to Us about God on Our Tour of the Grand Canyon

"You know that this was caused by the great flood, right?" The helicopter pilot informs us as we dip below the rim of the canyon, my heart dropping as we seem to almost kiss the green expanse of the Colorado. My husband replies with oh really, and I hadn't known that, and it makes sense, his hand gripping mine tight. "Yeah, it's a constant reminder of God's wrath." I want to laugh, but I don't. I breathe deeply, away from the headset mic, and concentrate on the truth passing before my eyes, the bands of colors, telling stories of epochs, life and destruction and life again, before mammals even existed. My husband politely grunts and the pilot takes it as agreement. "Yeah, the earth is only about six thousand years old, you know." I look at my husband, his eyes as wide as mine, and in that moment, we decide to stay quiet until we land in Vegas. "God made all of those fossils and put them in the ground for us to know his power." I try to focus on the vibration of the engine and not the rotors slamming into the side of the canyon. "I love this job. I get to see the wonder of God every day. It's the best church." I close my eyes, and I start to pray.

35mm

Every inch of the film from our wedding is sitting in a trash bag in the back of our closet. I wanted throwaway cameras and you insisted on 35mm film and rental Leicas on the tables as party favors, an expense I wasn't willing to give in to but you persisted, so I did. You were never worried that they might be stolen or damaged, losing us the sizeable deposit, which we could have used to just pay a damn photographer in the first place, but you wanted authenticity and truth. So now, we have cannisters of film in a black plastic sack on the floor of our closet, because you wanted to develop them yourself, but then you forgot, even though I remind you, again and again. I buy a kit to process the film into digital images, finally unveiling our wedding as seen through the eyes of our friends and family. The truth of us is captured in each frame, over and over again, making me wish I had left it all in the trash bag on the floor in the back of our closet.

Grogu Doesn't Need a Sippy Cup

Grogu chooses his ass-kicking space-faring father over the kooky religious space monk, green lightsaber flashing, past, present, future, across beskar chainmail.

We buy sippy cups as a joke, red wine on a white leather couch is not a good look, we joke to our friends online. I pose cute and yearning for wine, orange bears and yellow bees dancing in pink flowers in my grasping hands.

Grogu is older than his space dad but doesn't look it, able to float space rhinos and calm rampaging building-high beasts.

We build a shelving unit to hold all of your Legos. We decide to share our interests, your Millennium Falcon and Star Destroyer forever locked in battle below my ukuleles, a constellation of colors and sizes, hanging along the wall.

Grogu shares the trauma of war and genocide with his father, his kind, mainly children, slaughtered to protect a burgeoning empire, his own father a victim also, parents murdered by empire instructed droids.

We choose adventure, our lives entwined since childhood, escaping a life on an island too small for our galaxy of dreams.

Playing with Fire

We scramble across the street in Shibuya, our young bodies confined to matching school uniforms, jostled by salarymen and office ladies on lunch breaks, dressed in their own cloth prisons. We steer around retired obasans and ojisans, slow obstinate stones in the raging current. We escape from our fieldtrip group, filled with clueless boys and girls, our destination, a nest of K-pop shops feathered with purses, stickers, t-shirts, smartphone cases of our favorite idols. We drool over BTS, Twice, Blackpink, their braided lyrics of Korean, Japanese, English wind around us as we kakkoii and kawaii, rubbing their perfect faces, skin shining and almost translucent, their perfect bodies, dancer thin, against our bumpy skin and bulgy bodies. We race to eat army stew and tons of kimchi, daring each other to try the spiciest food on the menu, slurping up spam and fish cakes, noodles and rice, rap music scattering Korean like crunchy seaweed over us. We soak it all in, absorbing gochujang and gochugaru through our pores, our skins bursting open, revealing our new selves underneath, bodies sleek, skin pale, a fire raging in our bellies.

The Conveyor Belt Sushi Kat

lounges on her bed of vinegared rice, tucked under her tiny nori blanket. She's not exactly cozy but it's not too cold under the lights as she winds, round and round, the other plates of sushi, plucked one by one, by hungry customers. She's not sure if she wants to be chosen, her toe beans nibbled on by noisy children, drunken businessmen, harried mothers, and taciturn fathers. She watches their eyes darken as they see her coming, not really into the latest trend, like the sushi shop chain thought they would be. What better way to get rid of the stray cat population then to offer them to their customers? The conveyor belt sushi kat remembers a home once, warm and inviting, her every wish granted. They let her out one day on the side of the highway and never looked back. Now, she hopes maybe someone will choose her and take her home in a to go box, her body nestled in uneaten rice and pickled ginger.

Shinai

Your neighbor has got his shinai out again they say driving their car through his ghostly form, trailing vapors of former bamboo groves, dull blades dancing in dead breezes.

Your neighbor is laughing at us, they try to drive around him as he rides his shinai into the sunset, his cackles, blocking their way.

Your neighbor won't stop looking at us, his naked body pushed against the screen of his room's window, his shinai a dark length between his legs.

Your neighbor is sticking us with his shinai again, their bodies shimmering in the summer heat, steam rising, dumplings popping with each stroke.

Your neighbor won't let us through they say, windows rolling up, car inching forward, shinai rattling along the street.

The Reused Cool Whip Container

We all have special memories of the reused Cool Whip container, first bought for last year's Thanksgiving because no one wanted to buy heavy cream and make whipped cream from scratch. The double sized container was emptied of its luscious white fluff almost as soon as we cut our very first slice of store-bought pumpkin pie because no one could be bothered to make that from scratch either.

The Cool Whip container served us well for a year holding leftovers of Hamburger Helper, mac and cheese, chili, beef stew, taco meat, before crumpling in the sink after releasing the congealed mass of the meatloaf made by grandma for last Sunday's dinner.

It had lived next to the pots under the cutlery drawer, nestled in the multi-colored matryoshka of Tupperware mom had bought at a party she went to at the neighbors who served cocktail wieners cooked in grape jelly in a slow cooker.

We most fondly recall the day mom decided to make her famous green pineapple and carrot Jell-O salad in the reused Cool Whip container, because she had forgotten she had already used her only mold for a rum cake. The resulting wobbly tower sat jiggling on the table, the grooves of the container making decorative circles on top. It saved mom and for that we are eternally grateful.

We would also like to celebrate the life of the Reused Cool Whip Container with a moment of silence as we remember all of the times it also carried lunch for the kids, embarrassing them in the cafeteria.

The Reused Cool Whip container is survived by two Country Crock tubs filled with last night's goulash and the night before's spaghetti. We ask that in lieu of flowers that you please donate to our Save a Plastic Container fund we have created in memory of the Reused Cool Whip Container.

What if God Is One of Us

I saw God in the parking lot of a Taco Bell, temporarily closed after a viral video involving hot sauce and a waiting to be filled burrito. He was dealing coke out of the back of a souped-up Honda Accord, baggies bouncing to the beat of Handel's Hallelujah chorus on the subwoofers he had installed himself. He told me what if my name had been spelled d-o-g instead. I decided I didn't need anything he was selling.

The next time I saw God, it was a root beer colored dachshund, snuffling my crotch at my new neighbor's apartment. I had brought a bottle of wine as a housewarming gift, regretting my choice of Sauvignon Blanc. Not everyone likes the taste of cat pee, especially not a god lover, I mean dog lover. My neighbor told me she had gotten it at the shelter. Its name was God. Isn't that a hoot she giggled. I decided not to pet it and to get the hell out of that God-loving house before it tried to convert me.

I kept running into Gods everywhere I went. I just couldn't shake them.

She was the old Korean lady behind the register of the little grocery I popped into, scolding me over my purchase of an energy drink. Kimchi is better for your health. She shook her head at me as she handed me my change and a bag of free kimchi which I ate with my fingers on the sidewalk, the spicy fizzy garlic cabbage and carrots making me cry.

It was the broken payphone across the street from my apartment, the receiver dangling by a single wire, the droning tone conjuring memories of my mother who I hadn't spoken to in years, the graffiti on its side, a hodgepodge of what I assumed were Bible quotes but didn't have the courage to get any closer to read them. I wanted nothing more than to hang up that phone but I just couldn't bring myself to touch it.

They were the van living couple, draped in bohemian splendor, selling me crystals on the beach I decided to go to because I needed a break from all of the God sightings. You can feel the vibrations of the universe through these. They dangled slender pendants of pink, purple, black, blue, white, clear from leather coils over my head as I tried to relax. Live on another level they told me in chorus. I ripped those leatherbound rocks out of their hands, ran to the crashing waves of the Pacific Ocean, screaming, and threw myself in.

The final time I saw God, I walked right past, my existence unacknowledged, and for that, I was grateful.

Oh my god your voice sounds so haole

my cousin yells over the phone line as I call them up to see if they want to go drinking at our favorite bar when I come home to visit *how else am I supposed to sound I live on the mainland* I grumble at them *you think anyone going understand me if I stay talking like dis* they laugh *yeah yeah you still sound haole* I breathe and ask again *you like go Teru's for sing karaoke* they giggle and I know they just can't stop thinking about me living so far away and speaking as if I were better than everyone else *I bet you stay white as one ghost up dea* they just won't lay off *well stay hard for tan wen it stay snowing and I no like turn into one orange if I go in one tanning bed* I'm tired *you like cruise or what* they finish their fit *sure sure cuz no worries we going cruise* I worry I'm making a mistake *jus make sure you leave your haole high maka maka shit up dea, or else* the threat ringing in my ear as I hang up

Acknowledgments

"Trophies" first appeared in *Indiana Review*, Summer 2023, Volume 45, Number 1.

"The Black Box She's Only Seen on TV" first appeared in *Nostalgic AF: A Video Game Anthology*, June 18, 2021.

"daddy, he wen put limu in the fish's belly" first appeared in *The Rumpus*, April 24, 2023.

"Grover" first appeared in *Versification Misfit Micros November 2021*, December 1, 2021.

"The One Who Lies in Wait" first appeared in *New Flash Fiction Review*, September 27, 2021.

"Avon Calling You an Autumn When You Know You Are Summer" first appeared in *Milk Candy Review*, July 29, 2021.

"Far, Far Away" first appeared in *Cream City Review*, Spring/Summer Volume 47, Number 1.

"may day is lei day in Hawai'i" first appeared in *Cream City Review*, Spring/Summer Volume 47, Number 1.

"Menehune" first appeared in *Gigantic Sequins*, Issue 14 (June 2023).

"Cookies" first appeared in *Indiana Review*, Summer 2023, Volume 45, Number 1.

"go get da fish bat" first appeared in *The Rumpus*, April 24, 2023.

"Regret" first appeared in *Moon City Review 2024*, January 2024.

"A Ghost under the Kitchen Sink" first appeared in *(mac)ro(mic)*, November 5, 2021.

"Bitter over Sweet" first appeared in *The Rumpus*, April 24, 2023.

"The First Word" first appeared in *Bright Flash Literary Review*, June 2, 2021.

"The Devil You Don't Know" first appeared in *The Ilanot Review*, Spring 2024, March 12, 2024.

"Holoholo" first appeared in *Sledgehammer Literary Journal*, June 6, 2021.

"Wheel of Fortune" first appeared in *Maudlin House*, September 14, 2022.

"When the eye of Hurricane 'Iwa is passing over us" first appeared in *The Rumpus*, April 24, 2023.

"tangerine" first appeared in *FEED*, Issue 1.6, Spring 2020.

"to da lady who stay looking down her high makamaka nose at us" first appeared in *Pinch*, Volume 13, November 17, 2023.

"White wine spritzer" first appeared in *The Rumpus*, April 24, 2023.

"Cruising in Kona" first appeared in *swamp pink*, Issue 7, November 14, 2023.

"This Is Not Your Kind of Ghost Story" first appeared in *Hungry Ghost Magazine*, Issue One, Summer 2021.

"Lose 10 Pounds in 3 Days" first appeared in *Parentheses Journal*, Issue 14, Fall 2022, December 31, 2022.

"Planted in Blue" first appeared in *Bandit Fiction*, September 12, 2021.

"Black Coral" first appeared in *Claw & Blossom*, Issue Eight, March 21, 2021.

"Of Being" first appeared in *jmww*, January 20, 2022.

"Skin and Bone" first appeared in *Astrolabe*, December 21, 2022.

"Mother's Obake Shivers under Your Bed" first appeared in *Lost Balloon*, July 13, 2022.

"Tita's Sister's Boyfriend" first appeared in *The Argyle Literary Magazine*, March 15, 2024.

"Fishing for Akule" first appeared in *Superstition Review*, Issue 28, Fall 2021, November 30, 2021.

"You Should Never Eat Mangoes at Midnight" first appeared in *Subliminal Magazine*, Issue 2, October 23, 2021.

"For the Boy You Had a Crush on and Hoped Would Be under the Black Flap of Your Friend's Paku Paku" first appeared in *Complete Sentence*, June 12, 2021.

"Relax Said the Nightman" first appeared in *Newfound*, Volume no. 13, Issue 1, March 15, 2022.

"in ache" first appeared in *SmokeLong Quarterly*, Issue Seventy-Five, March 21, 2022.

"The Linebackers of Waikiki" first appeared in *Necessary Fiction*, July 21, 2021.

"Or Better Yet" first appeared in *The Cincinnati Review* miCRo series, July 19, 2023.

"As All Titas Do" first appeared in *Brown Bag Online*, Issue 4, December 21, 2021.

"To Ever Love One Girl" first appeared in *Milk Candy Review*, July 16, 2020.

"Where the Ali'i Are Hidden" first appeared in *Brown Bag Online*, Issue 4, December 21, 2021.

"Doing the Laundry" first appeared in *Fictive Dream*, August 28, 2022.

"Sacrament" first appeared in *Craft*, November 17, 2023.

"The Opihi Shell Necklace Hidden in My Mother's Closet" first appeared in *MicroLit Almanac*, May 9, 2024.

"Kona Boy Made Good" first appeared in *Milk Candy Review*, July 7, 2022.

"Oceans under Threat Like Never Before" first appeared in *Cheap Pop Lit*, April 21, 2022.

"Sweet Water" first appeared in *Empty House*, Issue Nine, December 29, 2022.

"Or Else" first appeared in *Five South*, September 20, 2022.

"We No Get Slopes" first appeared in *Waxwing*, Issue XXI, Summer 2020.

"And Nothing Else to Do" first appeared in *Flash Frog*, June 26, 2023.

"Once Upon a Time in Hawai'i" first appeared in *Astrolabe*, December 21, 2022.

"They Would Have Told You" first appeared in *Fractured Literary*, May 1, 2023.

"A Primo Place to Stay" first appeared in *The Citron Review*, Issue 10, Spring 2020.

"Coming Home" first appeared in *Reckon Review*, March 21, 2022.

"Giving All the Aloha" first appeared in *Ellipsis Zine*, July 5, 2023.

"Believe We Are Magic" first appeared in *The News Station Lit*, October 21, 2021.

"Crush" first appeared in *Emerge Literary Journal*, Issue 21, February 13, 2022.

"A girl" first appeared in *National Flash Fiction Day's Flash Flood*, June 18, 2022.

"Another Night on da Kona Pier" first appeared in *The Island Review*, June 23, 2020.

"The Mongoose" first appeared in *Hex Literary*, January 9, 2024.

"Principles of Lust" first appeared in *Rejection Letters*, November 1, 2021.

"All Wisdom Is Not Taught in Your School" first appeared in *The Hennepin Review*, April 2022 Issue, March 31, 2022.

"the graduation party you decided to skip" first appeared in *The Citron Review*, Summer Issue 2022, June 21, 2022.

"Stifling the Weeds" first appeared in *ANMLY #37 :: Future Possible*, October 31, 2023.

"the mongooses of Pahala" first appeared in *The Rumpus*, April 24, 2023.

"Living on Stilts" first appeared in *Craft*, November 17, 2023.

"Be Careful What You Wish For" first appeared in *Trampset*, December 9, 2022.

"The Day Captain Cook Missed Hawai'i" first appeared in *The Lumiere Review*, Party Time Issue, April 14, 2021.

"Paradise" first appeared in *Gooseberry Pie Lit Magazine*, March 21, 2024.

"The Cannibalistic Sea Slug" first appeared in *Anti-Heroin Chic*, February 5, 2022.

"Tweezer" first appeared in *Red Fez*, Issue 152, December 15, 2021.

"Fire and Sea" first appeared in *Fractured Lit's BIPOC Bittersweet Love Story Anthology*, October 23, 2023.

"This Is a Story about That Can of Tuna You Left on the Counter" first appeared in *The Cabinet of Heed Literary Journal*, Issue 47, June 1, 2021.

"How to Care for the Giant Hawaiian in Your Life" first appeared in *Sledgehammer Literary Journal*, July 9, 2021.

"The Helicopter Pilot Who Decided to Preach to Me about God on My Tour of the Grand Canyon" first appeared in *CafeLitMagazine*, June 17, 2021.

"35mm" first appeared in *Six Sentences*, August 9, 2021.

"Grogu Doesn't Need a Sippy Cup" first appeared in *Cotton Xenomorph*, November 1, 2022.

"Playing with Fire" first appeared in *The Razor*, June 1, 2022

"The Reused Cool Whip Container" first appeared in *Ruby Literary*, Issue One, June 3, 2022.

"What if God Is One of Us" first appeared in *Atlas + Alice*, August 11, 2022.

"Oh my god your voice sounds so haole" first appeared in *Craft*, November 17, 2023.

About the Author

Melissa Llanes Brownlee, a native Hawaiian writer living in Japan, received her MFA in Fiction from the University of Nevada, Las Vegas. Her work has been widely published in literary journals and magazines, including *The Rumpus, Cincinnati Review miCRo, Indiana Review, Craft, swamp pink, Moon City Review, Wigleaf* and others. She just learned to ride a motorcycle and you can find her driving through the Japanese countryside on the weekends. She doodles @lumchanfa and plays her ukulele at @lumchanukulele on Instagram. She also tweets @lumchanmfa and talks story at melissallanesbrownlee.com.

Also from Santa Fe Writers Project

Mona at Sea *by Elizabeth Gonzalez James*

This sharp, witty debut introduces us to Mona Mireles — observant to a fault, unflinching in her opinions, and uncompromisingly confident in her professional abilities. Mona is a Millennial perfectionist who fails upwards in the midst of the 2008 economic crisis.

"Mona at Sea is sharply written Millennial malaise that dares to be hopeful."

— Georgia Clark, San Francisco Chronicle

I'm Not Hungry But I Could Eat
by Christopher Gonzalez

Christopher Gonzalez's compact short story collection about messy and hunger-fueled bisexual Puerto Rican men who strive to satisfy their cravings of the stomach, heart, and soul in a conflicted and unpredictable world.

"Gonzalez works multiple registers, creating rich, compressed portraits of his characters. This is as poignant as it is hilarious."

*—*Publishers Weekly, *Starred review*

My Chinese America *by Allen Gee*

Eloquently written essays about aspects of Asian American life comprise this collection that looks at how Asian-Americans view themselves in light of America's insensitivities, stereotypes, and expectations.

About Santa Fe Writers Project

SFWP is an independent press founded in 1998 that embraces a mission of artistic preservation, recognizing exciting new authors, and bringing out of print work back to the shelves.

  @santafewritersproject |  @SFWP | sfwp.com